MW00879440

CHAPTER 1: STONE OF SISYPHUS

Blood, sweat, and tears trickled down his body as he used every ounce of his strength to push the enormous stone up the monumental mountain. However, each time he fought his way to the mountain's peak, the stone would roll back down to the bottom.

"According to Greek Mythology, Sisyphus was a king punished for deceit. The God Zeus cursed Sisyphus to roll a gigantic stone up a mountain for all of eternity, only to watch it always roll back down. He would be forced to roll the stone back up to the top, over and over again, for all of eternity." My World History teacher, Mr. Stevens, told us this while trying to talk with a creepy accent.

Sometimes, I felt he just liked to hear himself talk, but his message about Sisyphus was beginning to sink in. When he told that myth in my Junior World History class, never in a million years did I think that myth would soon symbolize my own life. I knew a little about the "Stone of Sisyphus" myth because of my favorite rock band, Chicago. Chicago is one of the most successful rock bands ever and has been a band since 1967. They had a long-lost album and song called "Stone of Sisyphus."

Although I was listening to Mr. Stevens, I never fully understood this myth until I hit one of the lowest points in my life. Like Sisyphus, we all roll an enormous stone up a mountain for eternity. Life is a series of ups and downs; everyone, no matter how rich or famous they are, will have their stone roll down at some point. The people who can roll their stone up the most are the winners. I knew that I was a winner, but there were many obstacles that I would have to overcome to prove that I was.

My name is Drew Russo, and I am a 5-foot-9 Italian-

American running back with brown hair and hazel eyes. I weigh roughly 175 pounds. My name Drew means "brave" and I tried my best to live up to my name. I played high school football for St. Andrews, a Catholic high school in Clarence, New Jersey. St. Andrews was a magnificent school that helped me learn about my Catholic faith and improve my work ethic, both academically and athletically.

I had been running hills, playing football, and lifting weights since I was six years old, but my "Stone of Sisyphus" never rolled all the way down the mountain until I was 17 years old. Ironically, the same day Mr. Stevens talked about the "Stone of Sisyphus," my first major setback would occur.

I was so excited about my upcoming senior football season because I had finished my third year of starting varsity for the St. Andrews Americans. Although there were some rough moments, I had three solid seasons with the team. I thought the upcoming season would be my breakout season, the season that would make me famous and separate me from the rest of the players. I truly felt like I was at the very top of the hill. I wanted to have the most outstanding senior football season and get a Division I football scholarship. But my optimism turned into pessimism that one March day when my world came crashing down on me.

That same day, after Mr. Stevens finished his speech on Sisyphus, the bell rang to signal the end of school. I quickly walked out of class and put my headphones on to blast Chicago's song "Stone of Sisyphus" since I had just learned about Sisyphus. As soon as I got outside, I put on my Prada sunglasses and walked to the bus. I got on the bus, and while listening to "Stone of Sisyphus," I envisioned myself as Sisyphus pushing up the immense stone. Although Sisyphus was not the most pleasant mythological character, his situation was one that almost everyone could relate to. The lyrics in the Chicago song stated, "A dream is make-believe until blood, sweat, and tears turn faith to will, it's gonna take some miracle man to show there's a away, I'm gonna take the Stone of Sisyphus, I'm gonna roll it back to you." I finally started to break down these lyrics while thinking about what Mr. Stevens said about Sisyphus.

In my mind, the lyrics meant that until you actually put all of your blood, sweat, and tears into achieving your dreams, then dreams are just fantasies. These lyrics inspired me to want to be that miracle man who turned his dreams into reality by working hard, and I knew that the night of our first spring practice was the right time to start.

I finally stopped daydreaming as the bus stopped a block from my house in front of a Catholic church called Immaculate Conception. I got off the bus and prayed at the Virgin Mary statue in front of the church. I always took about 5 minutes each day to focus and talk to God when I prayed. On my headphones, I put on Chicago's beautiful orchestral piece called "Prelude," knelt by the statue, folded my hands, and spoke to God mentally. I asked God to help the people who were in need, like the homeless and the sick children. I had been going to Catholic school since pre-school. My elementary school, Saint Raphael's, and high school, St. Andrew's, inspired me to focus on my Catholic faith daily.

After prayer, I switched the song on my iPod to the classic Chicago song "Does Anybody Really Know What Time it Is?" My parents raised me on the music of Chicago, and although it wasn't considered "cool" music anymore by the younger people, I did not care. I loved what I loved and did not care what anyone thought about me. I also watched a lot of the old television programs with my parents such as *Leave it to Beaver* and *I Dream of Jeannie*. I thought they had more class than the modern reality shows. I was never afraid to be myself and did not pretend to like something just to fit in. Listening to Chicago's vast music catalog always brought me back to when I was young; they were the soundtrack of my life. They were one of the first rock bands to have a horn section, and hearing their pretty melodies with the brass always made me smile. Chicago's music was much more melodic and classy than the modern music at the time as well.

The lyrics of "Does Anybody Really Know What Time It Is" matched my situation because, as Chicago's Robert Lamm sang, "As I was walking down the street one day," I was walking down the street of the city where I lived. I lived in the Chambersburg section of Trenton, NJ. Chambersburg used to be a predominantly Italian section of Trenton that had the best restaurants, but some of the Italians moved to the suburbs, and the area started to get more violent. My family still loved it, and it was our home. I always walked around the neighborhood, and I could smell the Italian Restaurants, such as the Roman Hall and Amici Milano, cooking their food.

The next Chicago song that played on my iPod was the majestic "Questions 67 and 68." This more upbeat song started with those incredible horns and Terry Kath's phenomenal guitar. When Peter Cetera's soaring tenor vocals began to sing, it inspired me to pick up my pace into a jog. I jogged past the legendary Italian Peoples Bakery and could smell the freshly baked bread. The two little Italian guys who always sat outside drinking their coffee yelled, "Yo, Drew." It made me feel good that my neighbors loved me.

Running around the Italian neighborhood made me feel like Rocky Balboa running around the streets of Philadelphia. I was a huge fan of Sylvester Stallone and his brother Frank. Frank Stallone's band Valentine lived in Chambersburg in the 70s and even played at my dad's high school prom. Sylvester Stallone's *Rocky* movies were my biggest inspiration because Rocky was a short Italian guy like me and was the ultimate underdog. Sylvester Stallone and his character Rocky beat all the odds to get to the top. Watching Rocky work out so hard made me want to work out like he did. After a 10-minute run listening to Chicago, "Gonna Fly Now," and "Take You Back" from *Rocky* and getting flashbacks of some of my best football moments while jogging, I went home to get ready for dinner with my family.

After dinner, I watched my Junior Football Season highlights with my father, and I was so excited that I was going to our first spring practice. My father gave me one of his traditional motivational speeches.

"This is it, Drew. It starts tonight. This is going to be your year. You have to work your absolute hardest to show you are the absolute best player there is. You have more heart, strength, and speed than anyone I know. You got this, son. I love you," my father told me with so much emotion and a slight tear in his eye.

"I promise I will work my absolute hardest, Dad," I told him and hugged him. I enthusiastically ran upstairs to get my spikes and gloves so my dad could drive me to an indoor turf field.

We arrived at the field, and after my team warmed up, we started doing pass patterns. I played slot receiver also so it was important that I practiced my patterns. I felt faster than ever, but the 4th pattern I ran drastically changed everything. Our quarterback, Andrew Brady, told me to run a down-and-out pattern, so I sprinted to the line of scrimmage and lined my right foot up to about an inch off the 50-yard line. I got down in my slot receiver stance and was ready to fly on the quarterback's left side. I was looking over at Brady and could not wait for him to say the cadence, which is the saying that the quarterback uses to signal to the other teammates to start the play in unison.

Brady slowly shouted, "Set, Ready," and as he said, "Hike," I exploded off the line of scrimmage as if I was running for my life. As soon as I reached 10 yards, I planted my right foot and was about to run a down-and-out pattern. A down-and-out pattern is when the receiver runs straight, and when he reaches his destination, he plants his inside foot into the ground, makes a sharp cut to the outside, and runs straight to the sidelines. When I attempted to make my cut to the sidelines, my foot did not want to follow me, and it got stuck in the field turf because I wore spikes. That moment felt like my world had just stopped. My right knee buckled, I heard a loud pop and felt excruciating pain. I fell to the turf like a ton of bricks, and my father came running over to me hurriedly.

In the back of my mind, I knew that it was a severe injury, but I did not want to believe it at first. I played football for 11 years and never missed a single game or practice. I was not about to let this injury keep me down. I attempted to get up, but it felt like a knife had just pierced through my knee. I knew I could not lie there and stay down, so I finally stood back up. I told my father I was okay and going back in, but he told me there was no way I would go back in.

I knew that he was right, and there was no use in arguing with him, but I felt like a baby because I got injured. My fellow players told me to feel better as Coach Reggie Smith gave me his infamous evil stare while I limped my way onto the bench. Smith was a 6-foot-3 ex-linebacker, former Marine and our Defensive Coordinator. He was very muscular and intimidating to the players, especially me. Smith, my dad, and I had a long history. He and my dad used to be close friends, but ever since I entered the school as a freshman, he tried making my life a nightmare. Smith had an ego the size of Texas and hated that I was quiet simply because he believed football players should be loud and obnoxious. Coach Smith threatened not to let me play in the past for reasons that did not make sense, but Coach McDuff always overruled him.

Coach Rich McDuff was the Head Coach, Offensive Coordinator, and Strength Coach. He usually backed me up and was on my side. Coach McDuff and my dad were also close because my dad was the St. Andrews head Freshman coach, scout, and filmer for our Varsity games. McDuff devoted his life to football and was an excellent old-school, class-act Coach. McDuff and Smith despised each other, but the Athletic director and Smith were cousins, so the school would never fire him.

McDuff's offensive players were more mannerly and quiet, and Smith's defensive players were usually loud and wild. There was little teamwork because the two coaches and their sides hated each other. The team often had several fights and arguments over the years. Coach Smith was always jealous of Coach McDuff because he wanted his jobs as the Head Football Coach and Strength Coach.

I lifted weights with Coach McDuff and my father. My father was the greatest dad in the world and did everything for me. My father worked two full-time jobs so my mom could stay home and raise us. On the weekdays, he was a Physical Education teacher, and on the weekends, he was a Flight Attendant. Not only did he do that, but he also created an entire football league for me and my brothers to play in. He also trained me with weights since I was six years old to accomplish my goal of becoming the best athlete I could be. We would exercise together like warriors, blasting our favorite Chicago Albums and *Rocky* Soundtracks. He always taught me never to give up, so it was tough when I got injured and had to stop practicing.

The car ride home from the field was pretty miserable. I had ice on my knee, and my dad was blasting one of my favorite Chicago songs, "Make Me Smile," to make me feel better. My dad was saying very comforting things to cheer me up as well. He always had a knack for knowing what to say to make me feel better, but this time, it was not working. He wanted to take me to the doctor right away, but I told him that I wanted to wait a week to see if the pain would stop. He agreed with me, although I could tell he was still worried. My father was a former football player with his share of knee surgeries, so I knew he was concerned. He said if the pain didn't stop, he'd take me straight to the doctor. I agreed although I prayed the pain would go away in just a few days.

I tried to listen to the pretty music to take my mind

off of my injury. Ironically, as we drove past Chambersburg's Columbus Park and saw the little children playing on the swings, Chicago's Terry Kath started to sing the lyrics, "Children play in the park, they don't know, I'm alone in the dark, even though." Although my dad did his best to cheer me up, I felt sad and alone, like the song's first verse. When Kath started singing the chorus about the girl of his dreams, I tried to think about my crush, Allison Hanson, the tall blonde Captain of the Cheerleading team. But I was in so much pain that even thinking about her still could not make me smile.

We finally arrived home and saw my MomMom and PopPop sitting on their porch. They were my mother's parents who lived a house away from us, and we loved visiting them every chance that we could.

We parked in front of them and my PopPop said his usual joke, "I hope Drew isn't here, oh hiya Drew," pretending not to see me.

Although the joke got old, it was still funny because he always said it, and we looked forward to hearing him say it every single time he saw one of us. I got out of the car, and they got worried when they saw me limping.

My MomMom in her loud Italian voice yelled "Oh no my baby is hurt. I told your father that football is dangerous."

My MomMom was overprotective, like Bobby Boucher's Mama in *The Waterboy.* I assured them I would be fine, even though I had no idea if I would.

Then my friend, Frankie Rossi, came walking by. Frankie was a 25-year-old man with a learning disability. He had extra huge eyeglasses and always wore Chicago the band shirts. He was the nicest person you could ever meet, and he loved walking around the neighborhood, even though it was not as safe as it used to be. Frankie loved watching me play football, and we even hung out sometimes. He asked me what was wrong when he walked by my house. I told him I got hurt playing football but would be alright. He then asked me if I had listened to Chicago that day, and I told him I did.

"I love Chicago," he said in his sweet high-pitched voice.

I then told him to hurry home because it was getting dark, and my family and I did not want anything bad to happen to him. My dad and I said goodbye to him, and then my dad helped me inside the house. Climbing the steep steps of my row home with my injured knee was very difficult, but I made it in successfully.

As soon as I got inside, I sat back on the lounge chair to elevate my leg. My dad got me more ice to put on my knee. I put on Chicago's beautiful instrumental pieces called "Canon" and "Once Upon a Time" because they were a bit depressing and fit the mood that I was in. But my dad wanted me to stop feeling depressed so he switched the song to "Stone of Sisyphus" and it sunk into my mind that my stone had fallen for the first time. I started to understand more about the myth. The lyrics to the bridge of the song were, "Looks like it's another one of those lonely nights, will we always be alone, that's never kept me from you, that's never stopped me from the fight." I felt depressed and alone like the song, but I knew that it was my time to fight the pain and roll the stone back up to the top. I was just terrified that I would not be able to overcome my current setback.

My mom came storming in like lightning to check on me. She was an incredibly nurturing Italian mother and housewife. She gave me a blanket because I was freezing and shaking from the ice. I was so nervous that I would not be able to play my upcoming Senior Football Season, but she put the blanket on me, kissed me gently, and told me how much she loved me. I was so grateful that I had such supportive parents who were always there for me.

My dad's name is Jimmy, and my mom's name is Mary-Anne. They were the best parents, who had been together since they were 14 and 16. Ironically, there was even a song from the 70s by the band Looking Glass called "Jimmy Loves Mary-Anne" and that was their theme song. My family did not have a lot of money but we were rich with love and always spent quality time together. My brothers Anthony and Michael also came over to me and told me that they hoped I would feel better. Anthony was 11, and Michael was 13 years old. They were both sweet and great younger brothers. I thanked my brothers for their support, and they told me that they would let me get some rest.

The next Chicago song that played was "King of Might Have Been," another one of my favorite songs, although the lyrics were undeniably depressing. It resonated with the situation I found myself in. Jason Scheff, Chicago's lead singer at the time, sang, "If this is what losing means, then I've lost everything, now I'm the king of might have been."

Tears streamed down my face as I truly felt like the "king of might have been." My thoughts weren't solely consumed by my injured knee; I also thought about my crush, Allison Hanson again, whom I was too shy to ask out. However, due to my knee, Allison became the least of my concerns.

After the song concluded, I folded my hands under my blanket and began to pray fervently. My prayers were twofold – for my knee to heal and for Frankie's safe return home. I continued to pray and cry, gradually crying and praying myself to sleep.

The next morning, I awoke with a scream, shaken by a nightmare. I dreamt I was Sisyphus, pushing a stone to the mountain's summit. Yet, my knee twisted, and the stone tumbled down on me. In my dream, I not only injured my knee but also tumbled down the hill with the stone. It was not just a nightmare; my stone had actually fallen because I was severely injured. I realized that I had a steep hill ahead, an uphill battle that I had to be prepared for.

CHAPTER 2: BABY, WHAT A BIG SURPRISE

The morning I woke up from my nightmare was a gloomy and rainy March day. My dad was driving me to school, and we were listening to Chicago's singer Jason Scheff's song "Hear Me Cry," and ironically, part of me wanted to cry due to how much pain my knee was feeling. Jason Scheff was my idol and I always loved listening to his music. We arrived at the school, and before I got out of the car, I told my father that I was feeling a little better and that I loved him.

Seeing his face through the rainy car window, I knew he could tell I was lying. I was still in terrible pain, and he knew it. He looked really worried, but I gave him a thumbs up as I limped my way into the school building.

Ironically, my crush Allison Hanson was walking behind me. Sadly, I was too shy to even talk to her, let alone ask her out. It was my dream to date her, but I had no confidence in my social skills because I was so different than the other kids. When she saw me limping, she asked if I was alright in her sweet, preppy, and high-pitched voice. I was embarrassed, but I told her it was just a minor injury and that I would be fine. She seemed sweet and even held the door for me. I thanked her in my very shy and soft voice and started to walk to my locker.

As I got to my locker, Thomas Simmons found me. Thomas had been in the same school with me since pre-school and was considered the biggest nerd in the school. He stuttered when he spoke, wore glasses, knew nothing about sports, and, unfortunately, was the laughingstock of the school. He always loved talking to me and followed me everywhere I went.

Although kids made fun of me for hanging with Thomas, I knew I had to be there for him. All the kids thought it was weird that I, the star running back, was always with such a nerd, but I had stopped caring what others thought of me. I knew Thomas had no other friends and needed me, even though it made me have no other friends because of it. So, I kind of gave up trying to have friends and girlfriends because Thomas was always around me.

I knew that as long as Thomas was always around, it would be impossible for me to have other friends or a girlfriend. It got to the point where I didn't even go to any of the dances because of him. When the other students were in the gym for the dances, I was down in the school basement weight room lifting weights with my dad and Coach McDuff. I was tired of the norm that athletes were expected to be obnoxious and make fun of nerdy kids. I figured that if the "cool" kids were not mature enough to be kind to Thomas, it was not worth having their friendship anyway. My dad raised me to not only be the best athlete but also the best person. I knew that I had the athletic ability and looks to be popular in school but if it meant having to break poor Thomas' heart to gain that popularity, it was not worth it to me.

Coach McDuff's speech during my first year also inspired me to be there for Thomas. Coach McDuff told this incredible story:

Three "cool" football players walking home from school saw a "nerdy" kid named Chris walking with a ton of books. Another kid tripped Chris, causing him to fall and drop all of his books. Chris was so embarrassed and was crying. Two of the "cool" football players laughed and kept walking. But one of the three, the star quarterback, walked over, helped Chris up, and asked if he was alright. Despite getting dirty looks from the other two players, the quarterback still went to help Chris. The quarterback helped Chris carry his books home, and they became friendly towards each other throughout the next few years. They were not best friends, but the quarterback always went out of his way to ask Chris how he was doing every time he saw him.

Years later, Chris became the valedictorian and had to give the speech at graduation. In the middle of the speech, he saw the quarterback in the audience and froze. He stopped speaking for a moment and pointed at the quarterback.

"That man over there saved my life. Three years ago, my world had hit rock bottom. My parents were getting a divorce, I got a bad grade on a test, and I had absolutely no friends. Then I was tripped by a bully, fell, and dropped all my books. I was planning on going home to end my life, but when this star quarterback reached down and helped me up, it changed everything. He walked me home and became my friend. I thought if this famous guy could be nice to me, maybe there was some light at the end of the dark tunnel. He saved my life. You never know how one act of kindness can save someone's life."

Coach McDuff shared this story every year, and every time he told it, I got choked up because it was always so emotional. I did not understand why it did not inspire the other guys on my team to treat the nonpopular kids with more respect. The story also made me think that maybe Thomas was my version of Chris, and I had to be the quarterback who saved him. I'm not saying Thomas had the same thoughts as Chris, but you never know what people are going through. That is why, no matter what, I always tried to be kind and give a friendly smile to anyone that I came in contact with. You never know how much a friendly smile can change someone's day from terrible to great.

Helping Thomas was also what Jesus would do. Jesus was not afraid to get rejected to spread His love. Unfortunately, in high school and sometimes even adult life, being good is not considered cool. But I did not care if people thought I was cool or not. I believed that being a hero was cool, and I kept being nice, always smiling and saying hello to anyone, especially Thomas.

But even without Thomas, I was different. I didn't curse,

drink, smoke, or listen to rap music. I had an old soul and focused on working out, playing football, and listening to my favorite oldie music. I had never even gotten one detention. I was a goody two shoes and proud of it. A lot of kids cursed and did bad things just to be popular and fit in, but I was never afraid to be myself. I did not care if I did not fit in with the "cool" kids. Unfortunately, peer pressure causes many people to do things that are harmful like being mean, and doing drugs and alcohol. I never wanted to do anything to harm my body because I wanted to be the greatest athlete that I could be. I knew that drugs and alcohol would destroy me, especially since I was still growing. I never gave in to any peer pressure. I was also very shy and quiet. I figured if being myself was not good enough to hang with the "cool" kids, then it was not worth hanging with them. I just stuck by Thomas' side.

Thomas and I were walking down the hall, and he did not even notice that I was limping. He was a friendly kid but was never interested in my life or football career. He just started talking about his upcoming Latin test, and I was in so much pain walking that I could not even pay attention to him. I just said, "Nice," and nodded occasionally to seem like I was interested. I didn't want to be mean, but I was really worried about my knee.

In the corner of my eye, I could see Allison and two other gorgeous cheerleaders walking to the side of me.

"There goes Drew and Thomas again," the one cheerleader said with a chuckle. It made me furious that they did not see me as being a kind person for being nice to Thomas. They just saw me as a weird guy.

Later at lunch, it was just Thomas and I at a table, like always. Thomas and I were only 2 of 3 people at Saint Andrews who went to Saint Raphael Elementary School. The other person was a sweet girl named Jenn, but she was always busy with her clubs and never had time for us. So, Thomas always sat with me, and I was not the type of person to tell him that he couldn't. I knew that he needed my friendship, and I had to be there for him.

Although I was a 3-year varsity football starter, people still wanted nothing to do with me as long as Thomas was around. Not even my fellow football players would sit with me. At first, it hurt, but then I realized how obnoxious many football players and athletes in high school were. Many of them thought they were better than everyone else, but I was raised to always be humble no matter how good or popular I became. I always remembered my Christian faith and tried to live as Jesus would. I wanted to be the best person that I could possibly be. Jesus was the greatest person who ever lived so I strived to be as much like Him as possible.

At first, it bothered me that Thomas was the only one around me, but I grew to like Thomas. We had nothing in common, but I started to see that Thomas was a great person. I wish more people saw Thomas for who he was inside instead of his nerdy exterior. I was also proud of myself for standing up for Thomas, especially when he got made fun of. My high school was very much about social statuses, cliques, and who had the most money and popularity. I always put people first and felt heroic for being a friend to Thomas.

It reminded me of the heroes I idolized as a kid. My dad always had me watching action movies about heroes like Hercules, Conan, He-Man, Rambo, and the Beastmaster since I was little, and I always wanted to be like those heroes. I wanted to be the muscular, athletic guy who helped people in need. So, befriending Thomas made me feel a little bit like my heroes. Unfortunately, these heroes like Hercules got all the girls, and I had never been on one date. I had never even kissed a girl before. I was too shy even to try to flirt with a girl.

Then something crazy happened that made me think that maybe my luck was beginning to change. Thomas had gotten up to get something to eat. As I was looking down at my football playbook, I heard multiple footsteps coming my way. I quickly looked up and was stunned to see that Allison and four of the prettiest cheerleaders in the school had come and sat next to me at my lunch table. I thought it had to be a dream or that maybe I died and went to heaven. I did not even know what to say. All I could hear was Chicago's 1977 hit ballad, "Baby What a Big Surprise" playing in my head because I was so surprised.

Then, the most remarkable thing happened. Allison Hanson asked if she could paint my number, 22, on her cheek during the next season's football games. I was so happy and quickly nodded.

I said nervously, "Yes, I would be... I would be honored."

She gave me a big smile and said, "Thanks, you are such a sweet guy! You made me so happy!"

I was stunned again. I had the biggest crush on this girl for three years, and yet I hardly even knew her. There she was, asking to wear my number on her beautiful face. She also told me that I made her so happy.

I wanted to tell her that she made me so happy, too, but I was so stunned that I froze. I tried to come up with words to say and was about to say that she made me happy too but then Thomas came back to the table. He was so shocked to see the girls that he tripped and dropped all his fries. The girls laughed, and Allison looked disgusted. The girls got up and obnoxiously left the table without even saying goodbye. I was so upset that Thomas had to come right when I was attempting to flirt, but I still found myself reaching down to help him pick up his fries. My knee was in so much pain when I bent down, but I was so excited about Allison that I did not give it much thought. Thomas apologized for how clumsy he was and asked if the hot girls had come for me.

I replied in a disgusted voice, "They were Thomas. They were. I'm not sure if they will ever come back, though."

Then he actually picked up a french fry off the floor and started eating it.

"Three-second rule," he said, which meant it was only on the floor for three seconds, so it was good to eat.

I gave him a weird look. He really had no idea they left because of him, but it was the story of my high school years. Every time someone tried to get close to me, Thomas came and scared them away. As much as it hurt, I knew that the Christian thing to do was to stay on Thomas' side, no matter how many French fries he ate off the ground.

Later that day, I could not stop thinking about Allison. I still had pain in my knee, but I was so distracted thinking about her. I thought there might be a possibility that she could want to date me. Why else would she say that I made her so happy and ask to wear my number on her cheek? I was so flattered, and at the end of the school day, we went to our Easter liturgy. Our school, Madrigal, sang some of my favorite Christian songs like "Here I Am to Worship" and "Lord I Lift Your Name on High" beautifully. I felt wonderful because of how upbeat the songs were and how excited I was that Allison was going to wear my number.

I prayed that God would give me the strength to overcome my injury and also the strength to ask Allison out. I also prayed that God would help Thomas find more friends. Even though I was annoyed at him for ruining my flirting opportunity, I knew he needed the prayers. I also knew that I had to stop being a coward and finally ask Allison out once Easter break was over. I was always waiting for a sign from her to show me that she liked me, and I finally believed I had one. I knew that only time would tell if she liked me the way I liked her.

CHAPTER 3: KING OF MIGHT HAVE BEEN

That night, I had another dream of pushing the stone back up to the top of the mountain. This time, Allison was helping me push it. Just as we were about to reach the top, I woke up. I kept having these dreams that had me going up and down the hill with the stone. I'm not a very good dream interpreter, but I believed they were showing me where I was. The dream gave me confidence that I would overcome the injury and get back to the top with the help of Allison and my parents' support.

On Holy Saturday, we spent the night with my father's parents and side of the family. They threw a grand party with an Easter egg hunt in their large den. Their den was so cool with a fireplace, big screen TV, and a 60s retro-style leather bar table. My grandparents were old but still had a great sense of humor. They were 81 years old, and I felt warm around them. My Pop was a hilarious man who loved to paint and tell jokes. My grandmother was the sweetest woman who always tried to feed me and give me money. Of course, my entire family asked about my knee when they saw me limping, but both my dad and I told them that I would be fine, even though we did not know what to believe.

I had so many mixed feelings. I was scared and nervous about my knee and about asking Allison out. I was still on a high about Allison flirting with me and always so happy to be around my family. I felt terrible because I did not even get to think about the most essential part of Easter Weekend: Jesus.

Fortunately, I did think about Him a lot on Easter in mass. My whole family went to mass on Easter at our church, Saint Raphael's. I took the time to thank God and Jesus for giving His life for us. Our priest's name was Father Stan, and he gave a very inspirational homily about Jesus and how He sacrificed Himself for us. He talked about all the pain He went through to prove to us that there is eternal life. I looked at the paintings of all The Stations of the Cross and saw all that Jesus went through and how he had to carry that huge cross. In some ways, the cross was like the stone, and Jesus kept moving forward despite falling and being in so much pain. I thought about how my knee injury did not even compare to the pain that Jesus felt. The homily motivated me to be more thankful for what Jesus did for us and not to feel sorry for myself.

I thought, "If Jesus could bear all that pain, then I could at least overcome a knee injury." Father Stan also said that despite all the horrible pain that Jesus endured, He knew that there was light at the end of the dark tunnel. He had something to look forward to, and that was eternal life.

Father Stan's speech inspired me, even though I was a little distracted by my father, who was coughing over the incense. When my dad finally stopped coughing, he noticed the pain in my face when I knelt.

He whispered, "Drew, I know you're still in pain. This Monday, I'm taking you to the doctor, and I won't take no for an answer," my dad said firmly.

"Fine," I said with an annoyed look on my face.

Then, my father continued to cough. "Oh boy, here we go again," I whispered to my mom as we shook our heads. The incense always bothered my dad.

A few days later, we were at the Trenton Orthopedic Doctors' office. Dr. Horton shook my hand and said it was nice to meet me. He was very kind, and I explained exactly what had happened to my knee. Dr. then noted that based on the description, I could have torn my ACL, and he wanted to give me the ACL touch test. When he gave me the Lachman touch test, he said it did not look torn, but he wanted me to get an MRI to see what was wrong.

A couple of days later, it was time for the MRI. I was a bit scared because I had never gotten an MRI before, and it looked kind of like a giant coffin. They let me listen to music, so I put on one of my favorite Chicago love songs, "You Come to My Senses." To distract myself from the MRI, I dreamt about Allison wearing my number on her face as I was listening to the gorgeous Chicago love song. Before I knew it, the MRI was finished, and they said that I'd get my results back in a day or two.

The next night, I sat on my couch watching my favorite Chicago live DVD, and my parents sat at the dining room table. They were whispering to each other and acting very strange. I quickly stopped my DVD and asked, "What is happening?" I asked them in an angry tone.

My parents shared a concerned look. My father walked over, sat beside me, and nervously said, "Drew, I have some bad news. The MRI results came back. I'm so sorry, but you have a completely torn ACL."

I was in shock, and tears started to flow down my face. I was so angry and sad that I tossed the DVD remote in my hand across the living room. I opened the door and stormed out of my house. My dad tried to follow me, but I took off walking down the street, and he told my mom to let me have some space. I put on my headphones and listened to some of the saddest songs, such as "Mickey" from *Rocky III* and Chicago's "P.M. Mourning." A part of me just wanted to give up, but then my friend Frankie came walking by and changed my thinking a little.

"Drew, what are you doing out here at night? Are you crying?" He asked concerned.

"Hi, Frankie. Yeah, I found out that I hurt my knee terribly, I told him in a crying voice.

"I'm sorry, Drew, but you are a hero of this town. Don't give up. All of Chambersburg believes in you. You are our Italian Stallion Champion like Rocky is to Philly," Frankie told me with so much emotion.

"Frankie, that means so much to me. I promise you, I won't give up. How about I treat you to some Italian ice?" I asked him.

"You bet," he said excitedly.

We then walked to the Panorama Musicale, the shop where the little older man named Pasquale from Italy would make the best homemade Italian Ice you could find. Frankie and I sat there eating ice and discussing our favorite Chicago songs and *Rocky* movies. I played one of Frankie's favorite Chicago songs, "Saturday in the Park," for him. We even started singing along. Even Pasquale joined in on the singing and sang the part, "a man selling ice cream singing an Italian song." Hanging with Frankie and eating the ice made me feel so much better, but I knew that when I went home, I would still have to deal with the devastating news again.

I then walked Frankie home because our neighborhood was getting dangerous at night. There were reports of violent gangs that were making their way into Chambersburg, so Frankie walking alone at night always concerned me. Once I got Frankie home safely, I put on "The Final Bell" from the *Rocky* soundtrack and jogged my way back home on my injured knee, which was feeling much better, considering the recent diagnosis. I was still furious, but at least I was determined to overcome the obstacle.

I soon found out that my parents knew the results two hours before they told me. My parents were terrible at telling me bad news, but I knew it wasn't their fault. I was just so angry that I took it out on them. When I walked back into the house, my mom started to sing the theme song from one of my favorite shows, *Friends*.

"I'll be there for you when your knee starts to hurt," she sang poorly while changing the lyrics to relate to me.

She was trying to cheer me up and make me laugh, but I

just looked at her and said, "Stop."

I asked my dad if I could still play my Senior football season, and he told me that we just have to see what the Doctor says. He told me he would do whatever it takes for me to play the season. He also told me not to tell a soul that my ACL was torn because the Coaches might not want to play me if they found out. I promised him that it would stay a secret until I heard what Dr. Horton had to say. I had an appointment with Dr. Horton in 2 weeks to see what we could do.

That night, I had another nightmare. I was rolling the stone close to the top with Allison, but then she just left me stranded to push the stone alone. The stone pushed me back down, and I was in so much excruciating pain that I could not push the stone back up. I tried hard to keep pushing it up but was not strong enough. It was one of those dreams where I felt like I was falling, and when I tried to let out a scream in real life, nothing came out. It was so terrifying, and when I finally was able to scream, it sounded like it came from a baby because it was so high-pitched. My dad came running in and hugged me.

"Drew, you are a fighter and a winner. You can overcome anything that stands in your way," he said as he hugged me tight.

I already had terrible news about my knee, so I knew that I had to have good news with Allison. I needed some positivity in my life and I was hoping that Allison would not leave me like she did in my nightmare. In the morning, I finally summoned the courage to approach Allison in the hall and asked her to hang out. I waited for Thomas to go to his Latin class and slowly approached Allison.

"Um, Allison?" I said.

"Oh hey, Drew! What a surprise! What's up?" She said with excitement.

"I was wondering if maybe...uh...maybe I can buy you lunch during activity period today?"

She said yes and thanked me in such an enthusiastic voice. I wanted to jump for joy.

"Awesome! I'll see you later!" I said enthusiastically.

As she walked away, I could hear the Chicago song "Victorious" in my head because I felt victorious that she said yes. I was so distracted that I bumped into Shane Hitt, my team's starting linebacker.

"Keep your eyes on the field, Russo. You better run the football next year better than you walk," he said obnoxiously, giving me a dirty look before walking away.

Hitt was one of Coach Smith's favorite players. He was an obnoxious rich boy who treated girls like trash. He cursed a lot and drank, but what baffled me was that Coach Smith actually liked him. Hitt also dated the prettiest girls in the school. I could never understand why the girls liked him. He was such a jerk, and he hated me because I bench-pressed and squatted more weight than him.

I went to my English class, and we watched the movie *Romeo + Juliet* with Leonardo DiCaprio. I just kept imagining that I was Romeo and Allison was Juliette during the kissing scenes. Every minute or so, I kept checking the clock. I felt like I was getting ready for a huge football game because I was so excited that I finally had a date, but I was so nervous because it was my first date ever.

The great thing was that I did not have to worry about Thomas interfering because he would be at his Latin club. He made me help him one day in there, which was one of my life's most horrifying experiences. Every person spoke Latin the whole time, and they were playing with action figures and beanie babies for some reason. I told myself that I'd never step foot in that room again. It gave me nightmares for a month. I was so glad that Thomas would be in there that day so that I could have my date in peace. I did come to care for Thomas but also needed some time to help myself. I felt like I deserved a chance to be with the girl of my dreams, Allison Hanson.

English class was finally over, and I walked to the cafeteria as if I was walking to the line of scrimmage. My leg was feeling much better, despite my torn ACL. I walked faster than I had in a while because I was so excited. When I entered the cafeteria, I stood in the corner and looked all over for Allison, but she was nowhere to be found. I even looked over at her usual table; every pretty cheerleader except for Allison was there. My heart started to beat extremely fast, and I made excuses like "Maybe she didn't finish a test, or maybe she was helping a teacher do something."

But all my excuses stopped when I saw her in line buying food with Shane Hitt while holding his hand.

I felt like I had just been hit 15 yards in the backfield by a 300-pound lineman. I slowly walked over and heard Shane say, "Let's go to the courtyard, Allison."

Then, my heart felt like it was ripped out and shattered into a million little pieces. Suddenly, I felt a tap on my back, and when I turned around, it was Thomas. "My Latin club is canceled. Wanna go to the courtyard with me?"

"Great... just great!" I thought to myself.

"Oh, Drew, I..I..I forgot my lunch money at home. Can you buy me lunch?" He asked while stuttering, and I told him that I could.

It could not have gotten any worse. First, I found out that I had torn my ACL. Then I got a date with Allison Hanson, only to get stood up on the same day so she could go out with the biggest jerk in the school. Then I had to use the 10 bucks my dad gave me for Allison for Thomas. Thomas and I sat alone on the bench while he was stuffing his face with his chicken fingers. He was making weird noises as he inhaled each chicken finger, which grossed me out immensely.

The worst part was that I had a great view of Allison and Shane right in front of me on their bench, and they were flirting and hugging up a storm. I had hit rock bottom. Here I was, sitting with the biggest nerd in the school who was scarfing down his food while I was watching the biggest jerk in the school have the date I was supposed to have with the girl I was infatuated with. I could not understand why she did that to me and why all of the heartbreaking stuff was happening to me. I knew I was such a good guy, and I just could not understand why the good guys lost so much, and the bad guys won.

I was in tears, and Thomas was too into his food to even notice that I was sad. I put on my headphones and started listening to Chicago's sad song "King of Might Have Been" because the lyrics defined the situation, like when I hurt my knee. "Oh, it's really over now, and I've got to live without the love I'll never have again; if this is what losing means, then I've lost everything; now I'm the King of might have been." I truly felt like the man in that song again because not only did I tear my ACL, but I lost Allison. Thomas was mumbling something in between each chew, but I was too upset to try to understand him. I was blasting the song and crying softly. I did not know where to look because Shane Hitt and Allison were getting romantic ahead of me, and next to me was Thomas Simmons wolfing down his chicken fingers. I just looked at the sky and prayed that God would help my life improve.

When the bell rang to end lunch, I saw Hitt and Allison kiss, and the kids yelled, "Ooooh." They screamed so loud that I could hear it over the Chicago music blasting from my headphones. It was one of the most heartbreaking moments of my life. My heart sank so low and fast, like the elevator from Disney World's Tower of Terror.

I finally got up and walked slowly. I could see Allison walking beside me, and I began playing Chicago's powerful number 1 song of 1989, "Look Away" on my iPod because the lyrics resonated with my situation: "If you see me walking by and the tears are in my eyes, look away baby look away, and if we meet on the street someday and I don't know what to say, look away baby look away, don't look at me, I don't want you to see me this way." The power of the guitar solo in the song and Bill Champlin's soulful vocals singing the lyrics made me cry even more. Luckily, she did not see me in tears. It has always been one of my favorite songs, but I never wanted to experience what the man felt in the song. It was heartbreaking.

When I arrived in Writing class, our assignment was to write a poem or a song about anything we wanted. Heartbroken and devastated, a song flowed out of me. It was about Allison and how she broke my heart. I made up some parts to make it flow, titling the song "Shattered" because she shattered my heart. Despite knowing nothing about music, the lyrics and melody just came to me. I started writing in my notebook:

"Shattered"

Verse 1:

I used to dream that I would be with you forever

I got butterflies every time we were together

I never knew it would end so badly in this ice-cold weather

After all I did for you, after all that we've been through

I never knew that you could leave me

Chorus:

So heartbroken, devastated, sobbing in the freezing snow

I can't believe you hurt me so

Left me so abused, feeling so confused

I can't believe you made me feel so flattered

And now you left me all alone, with my heart shattered

Verse 2:

I devoted my entire life to you, and I was there for you

Every time you try something new

I spent countless hours helping you

There wasn't a thing I wouldn't do

But then suddenly, you abandoned me

Without even thanking me and left me

Chorus:

So heartbroken, devastated, sobbing in the freezing snow

I can't believe you hurt me so

Left me so abused, feeling so confused

I can't believe you made me feel so flattered

And now you left me all alone, with my heart shattered

Bridge:

I just want to see you one more time

So I could give you a final goodbye

Chorus:

So heartbroken, devastated, sobbing in the freezing snow

I can't believe you hurt me so

Left me so abused, feeling so confused

I can't believe you made me feel so flattered

And now you left me all alone, with my heart shattered

My teacher loved the song, and I got a 100 on it. Despite the good song, I did not think I could ever put my shattered heart back together. But I was dead wrong. My heart would soon be mended that same day.

CHAPTER 4: LOVE WILL COME BACK

When the last-period bell rang, Thomas tracked me down again. He had this humongous science project that I had to help him carry. With my giant backpack on, my gym bag, and Thomas' project in my hands, I couldn't have felt any worse physically and mentally. I had my headphones on, listening to Chicago's "Chasin' the Wind" because the lyrics resonated with my situation. "Cause you can't really say it's over when it never has begun, no use making you care about me, no way that I'm gonna win, oh darling, I might as well be chasin' the wind." The song was about a guy who said he might as well be chasing the wind rather than trying to get the girl to like him – exactly how I felt about Allison.

Between my aching knee and my broken heart, a part of me just wanted to lie down and give up. I didn't think there was any light at the end of my dark tunnel, but I had no clue that everything would change in a second. The next song on my iPod was the epic Chicago and Rascal Flatts power ballad "Love Will Come Back." The two bands sang, "Another one is waiting there for you to open, if you believe, love will come back, and hit you when you least expect, fill in the cracks of the broken heart you thought that you could never mend, you can start again." As optimistic as the lyrics were, I knew it would not happen for me. I was so wrong. Carrying so much, I dropped my gym bag on the ground. Little did I know that dropping a gym bag could be the best thing to ever happen to me.

I bent down to pick up my gym bag and when I looked up, my eyes met a pair of gorgeous brown eyes staring right in front of me. These eyes belonged to Stephanie Marino, who had bent down to help me pick up my bag. For some reason, I never realized how gorgeous her eyes were under her glasses. She was beautiful with dirty blonde hair like Jennifer Aniston. Although we had never talked before, she seemed like a lovely girl and was a junior in high school like me.

Mesmerized by her beauty, I just zoned out and listened to my iPod play the next song, which once again fit the moment. The song was Chicago's "Someone Needed Me The Most," and the lyrics were, "When your heart reached out to me, I was there to hold it close, to be counted on for sure when someone needed me the most, I had someone to protect, lift them up when they got low and it brought us both to life when someone needed me the most."I then realized that I was daydreaming and hit the stop button on my iPod.

"Thanks, Stephanie. That is sweet of you," I said.

"You're welcome. You can call me Steph. I know we don't know each other well, but are you okay, Drew? You seem a bit down," she asked.

She could sense the heartbreak on my face. I shared that I had a rough day but reassured her that I would be okay.

Steph helped me walk Thomas to his bus and even carried one of his things. After Thomas left, Steph and I talked some more.

"It's really nice that you hang with Thomas," she said. "Are you two best friends?" She asked.

"Well, I went to school with him since preschool, and he was always picked on. I feel bad for him. He always talks to me, and I know he needs a friend. I do think he is a nice person. We just don't have a whole lot in common other than going to the same grade school. I know you probably think I'm weird like everybody else," I told her shyly.

"No way. I think you're sweet. It's very kind that a football star is willing to hang out with someone like Thomas. I wish every famous athlete was as humble and down to earth as you are," she said.

I thanked her, and we started getting to know each other on the bench while waiting for our parents to pick us up because both of our buses were late. She loved basketball and was the starting point guard for the girls' varsity team. She told me that she loved rock music, and I told her that I liked it as well. I shared that my favorite band was Chicago and discovered she only knew a couple of their songs.

I let her listen to my favorite Chicago songs, which she loved. The first Chicago song that I played for her was my favorite, and it was called "Will You Still Love Me?" I gave her one of my earbuds, and when the part where Jason Scheff sang "Two Hearts Drawn Together Bound by Destiny" came on, we both shared a passionate look. A part of me wondered if Steph was my destiny and not Allison. I also played her the new Chicago song at the time, "Long Lost Friend," and it felt like she truly was "my long lost friend that I lived for all my life, a gentle hand, a part of me that I was dying to find."

Steph and I hit it off and exchanged cell phone numbers. I had just gotten a cell phone, so when she started texting me, it was the first time I ever texted a girl my age. We texted each other all night, and although she was not a famous cheerleader like I thought I would date, deep down inside, I was falling in love with her. She was the first true best friend that I ever had, and I felt like I finally found a person my age who understood me. She was also Italian, and we shared old-school values. She was not into drinking or cursing and was highly respectful like I was. We started hanging out a lot at school, and for a while, I was so happy that I forgot all about the torn ACL and the Allison disaster.

Thomas had been occupied with his clubs, so Steph and I got to hang out more. I even opened up to her about what happened with Allison, and I wanted to tell her about my torn ACL too, but I knew I had to wait. For the first time in a while, I was excited to go to school to see Steph. I even told my parents all about Steph, and they could also sense that I was falling for her, but I was too shy to admit that to them.

When my dad was taking me to school one day, he tried to talk to me about Steph.

"You know, Drew, just because Steph is not a popular cheerleader doesn't mean you can't date her," he said confidently.

I quickly cut him off and told him that we were just friends and that I was just focused on my injury. But I knew that he was right.

Steph and I hung out on the first Saturday of May. I introduced her to my parents and my favorite shows, *Seinfeld and Friends*. She had never seen *Seinfeld* before, and she had the cutest laugh. After several *Seinfeld* episodes, I couldn't resist putting my arms around her. She seemed so happy that I did, too.

Seinfeld had just ended, and we looked at each other very close in the eyes. I put on the Chicago love song "We Can Last Forever," and I asked her if I could do something. She told me that I could, so with the arm that wasn't wrapped around her, I took her glasses off and was amazed at how even prettier her eyes were without her glasses.

"I love seeing your beautiful eyes without glasses," I told her.

With a blushing face, she thanked me. I wanted to kiss her so badly, and we both leaned in. Chicago's Jason Scheff sang, "Don't ask me why, 'cause I don't even know how I gave you my heart, I gave it all to you, now there's no way that I can lose." Just as the song's chorus was about to kick in, our lips were about to touch. Then, all of a sudden, my parents came in with the food.

"Who's having chicken?" My dad said in his goofy voice while giving my mom the bag of fried chicken.

I quickly backed up right before we were about to kiss.

"What's going on in here?" My mom asked suspiciously, and my dad was just in a rush to use the bathroom.

He did not even notice and ran upstairs quickly screaming "Gotta go to the bathroom." Steph and I laughed at him.

"That was close," I whispered to her.

The rest of the night was a bit awkward. We knew we were both falling for each other, but neither could admit it. My parents drove Steph home, and we blasted the Chicago songs "Runaround" and "Man to Woman" in the car. My dad tried to sing the high parts of "Man to Woman" sung by guitarist Dawayne Bailey, but he sounded like a dying cat. Steph and I were cracking up. Despite my dad's atrocious singing, I truly felt the lyrics of "Man to Woman." When Jason Scheff sang, "Hold me close, you're the nearest thing to heaven that I know, I could feel the fire that burns inside you, look how this love has grown," I held Steph tight and genuinely felt like I was in heaven. My mom saw me through the mirror and gave me a funny look. We finally got to Steph's house, and she thanked me for a magnificent night. We hugged each other, and she invited me over the next night.

The next night I met her mother and we cuddled on the couch. I brought one of my favorite '80s movies, *Masters of the Universe*, starring one of my idols, Dolph Lundgren, to show Steph. It was also one of Courteney Cox's first movies. I don't know what I was thinking because it was a cheesy action movie from the '80s. I don't know why I thought Steph would have liked it, but I liked it, and it may have been my good luck charm.

When her mom went out, I muted the movie and put on one of my favorite Celine Dion songs, "I Surrender." I put my arm around her again, and we stared into each other's eyes. "

So what would you do if I kissed you?" I asked her. She blushed and smiled. "I want to, but then again, I don't want to ruin our friendship," I said.

Then she confessed that she had a crush on me since freshman year. I felt so bad because I had never even noticed her. We both paused for a minute, and I again removed her glasses. I started to lean in for a kiss, but I stopped myself. I sighed and thought about it for a minute.

"Oh, I'm going for it," I said, then kissed her right on the lips.

With the passionate Celine song playing in the background and feeling my lips on hers, I got chills as it was one of the most magical moments of my life.

Once we started kissing, we could not stop. When we finally managed to break apart, I laughed. "I never thought my first kiss would be during *Masters of the Universe*. It's so romantic, and Billy Barty makes me wanna kiss you more." Steph was cracking up because Billy Barty was a little character named Gwildor in the movie. She laughed so hard but before long, we started kissing again. The night eventually had to end, but I knew it was "only the beginning" of a fantastic relationship between Steph and me.

We decided to officially be boyfriend and girlfriend that night. I told my parents about our relationship, and they were ecstatic but, of course, annoying. My mom wanted to know if I kissed her. I did not answer her, but my huge smile gave it away. They both hugged me and told me how happy they were for me. Then my brothers teased me, and Anthony sang "Drew and Steph sitting in a tree." I just laughed and continued texting Steph.

A couple of hours later, we were both getting sleepy, so she sent me a goodnight text on the phone, and I sent one back to her. I laid down in bed and just kept picturing her beautiful face. I kept replaying our first kiss over and over in my head. I had never been happier yet was mad at myself for chasing the wrong girls for so many years.

In a way, I was a hypocrite. I always hated how kids in my school only cared about people's social statuses and popularity. But I just began to realize that I was no better. I only cared about dating a popular cheerleader for so many years instead of the sweet and beautiful Steph. If I was not so worried about dating the popular girls, I could have noticed Steph sooner.

But like my dad always told me, "I couldn't be a Monday morning quarterback."

That meant I couldn't go back to the past and change things. I just had to look forward to the future, and Steph gave me so much to look forward to.

I had trouble sleeping that night because my heart was so excited that it felt like it had wings and was flying. I kept picturing Steph's gorgeous brown eyes when she bent down to help me pick up my gym bag that first day I got to know her. That moment inspired me to get out a piece of paper and write another song called "Paradise in Your Eyes."

Like I said before, I knew nothing about music or singing, but I was decent at writing lyrics and vocal melodies. Like "Shattered," which I wrote about Allison rejecting me, this song just came to my head. It was all about my love for Steph and how I felt when I gazed into her eyes. But I did not want to share it with her right away. I wanted to take singing lessons to surprise her one day and sing it to her. I saved the song on my computer until I learned how to sing. In my Microsoft Word document, I wrote this title:

"Paradise in Your Eyes"

Verse 1:

Girl, your eyes are so gorgeous and bold

They make me feel warm when I'm freezing cold

Girl, your eyes are so sweet and so brown

I could stare at them all night without even making a sound

Now it's time to tell you how I feel every time I look at you

Chorus:

I was so lost for most of my life

But ever since I met you, everything feels so right

Oh I promise to be always by your side

Cause every time I look at you

I can always see paradise in your eyes

Verse 2:

Girl, your smile is so pretty, so heavenly

Every time I see you, feels like heaven to me

Girl, your hair is so beautiful and long

Every time I'm with you, I always feel so strong

This is how I feel every time I look at you

Chorus:

I was so lost for most of my life

But ever since I met you, everything feels so right

Oh, I promise to be always by your side

Cause every time I look at you

I can always see paradise in your eyes

Bridge:

I was a lost soul wandering through this life

Always searching for that Mrs. Right

But then you came to me so unexpectedly

You're my best friend and will be my lover till the very end

Chorus:

I was so lost for most of my life

But ever since I met you, everything feels so right

Oh, I promise to be always by your side

Cause every time I look at you

I can always see paradise in your eyes

CHAPTER 5: MAKE A MAN OUTTA ME

Although I felt like I was living in paradise with Steph, there was still one major setback that I needed to overcome: the fact that I had a torn ACL, and my senior football season was less than five months away. My dad and I finally returned to Dr. Horton to discuss the injury.

Dr. Horton entered with a few papers and a dejected look.

"Okay, so you know it's a complete torn ACL. It's a severe injury, and I recommend that you get surgery as soon as possible," he said with a concerned expression.

"But it's my senior football season next year," I explained nervously. "If I get the surgery, would I be able to play football next year?"

I could see him wince. "Unfortunately, it is a 9—to 18-month recovery, so I'm afraid you will have to miss your senior football season. I'm sorry," he said.

"Can't I play with a torn ACL?" I asked, trying to fight the tears rolling down my eyes.

My dad chimed in, "Doctor if he got a brace, would it be possible for him to play with a torn ACL?"

The Doctor turned to my dad with the same sorrowful look. "I'm sorry, Mr. Russo, but there is a zero percent chance that a running back could play football with a torn ACL. With all the cutting, twisting, turning, and getting hit, he can risk damaging his knee more drastically. Luckily, you have not had any damage to your meniscus yet. If you damage your meniscus, Drew, you may never be able to play football again. Or worse, you may never even be able to run again. I highly suggest that you get surgery, but it's your decision," he said sternly.

"But...I don't even have any more pain..." I said in a

mournful voice.

"I'll admit, Drew, that you have the strongest leg muscles I have ever seen. Because your legs are so strong, I could not tell that your ACL was torn from the touch test. Most people who have torn ACLs can hardly walk, but it is still an ACL tear, and it is impossible to play an entire football season with it torn," he continued. "I do not believe anyone in the world has ever done it before."

Every fiber of my being recoiled from his words. I turned to my dad. "I still want to try to play. Please, Dad?"

My dad sadly looked at me. "Drew, are you sure you want to risk never being able to run again just for one season? I lost all of my menisci, and I can never run well again. I had six knee surgeries, and I don't want to see you end up like me in 20 or even five years, but it's up to you. I will support and stand by you with any decision you make."

"Dad, I know what you are saying, but I worked my whole life for my senior season. This is the most important season of my life. I can't miss it. Please help me?" I begged him.

He hesitated, but finally, he nodded. "Of course, son. You will not miss your senior football season. We will get a brace, Doc, and try to do the impossible. This kid has so much heart; if anyone can do it, it is him."

My dad did so much for me, but that moment just made me feel so awesome to know that he had my back, or in that case, my knee. I didn't know what I would do without him. We both thanked the Doctor and shook his hand. Still, he gave me that stern warning.

"I respect your decision, but I strongly oppose it. I hope you prove me wrong. Let me know when you want to come back and schedule your surgery," he said.

We thanked him again and went out to try and get a knee

brace. As we waited for the guy to come out with our knee brace, I kept thinking about what Dr. Horton said, which was ingrained in my memory.

"It is impossible to play football with a torn ACL."

I kept hearing it over and over again in my head. When I finally noticed my dad calling out my name, I apologized.

"Sorry, Dad. I was thinking about this whole situation. I will prove Dr. Horton wrong and play the entire football season with a torn ACL. Like Rocky went the distance with Apollo Creed in his first fight, I will go the distance with a torn ACL. I vow not to miss one game. Better yet, I vow not to miss one practice," I told him.

I had so much confidence, and I believed I could do it with my family's and my girlfriend's support. The thing was that I had not even told Steph yet.

My dad sighed. "Drew, if you're going to do this, you must always wear your brace at all times. Most importantly, you cannot tell anyone. If Coach McDuff or Smith discovered you had a torn ACL, they would never play you. Even worse, if the other team found out, they would try to take out your knee and put you on the sidelines permanently," my dad told me with a nervous look on his face.

"We're gonna work harder than we ever worked in the weight room and build up your surrounding leg muscles."

I thanked my dad for always being on my side, and we hugged each other tighter than the knee brace would fit on my knee. One of my dad's favorite Chicago songs was called "Make a Man Outta Me," and it was about how having a son made a man out of the father and changed his life. My dad always told me that my brothers and I made a man out of him. But I thought it was the opposite because my dad made a man out of me, and I did not know what I would do without him. The gentleman ended up coming back with the knee brace, and it was a perfect fit. I was ready to try to do the impossible and play football with a torn ACL.

The next night, my parents, Steph, and I saw the new and 6th *Rocky* movie, *Rocky Balboa*. My dad had shown me Rocky movies since I was just a baby, and they have played a massive role in my life. One scene in the new film inspired me more than any other scene. In the scene, Rocky's son is lost and depressed. Rocky found him and said, "Life ain't about how hard you can hit. It's about how hard you can get hit and keep moving forward. How much you can take and keep moving forward. That's how winning is done." My dad and I looked at each other with tears dripping down our faces and nodded because we knew the quote related to our current situation. I knew I had fallen and would fall again, but I had to keep getting up and moving forward. My dad was my Rocky to me and always gave me inspirational talks.

That night, my dad took me to my attic bedroom/weight room, and we started working out my surrounding leg muscles harder than ever with my knee brace on. We were blasting "No Easy Way Out," "Hearts on Fire," "Burning Heart," and "The Sweetest Victory" from the *Rocky IV* soundtrack. I listened to the soundtrack my entire life, but the lyrics started to relate with me. In Robert Tepper's "No Easy Way Out," the chorus states, "There's no easy way out, there's no shortcut home," and I knew there was no easy way out of the situation. In Survivor's "Burning Heart," the words "In the warrior's code, there's no surrender, though his body says stop, his spirit cries, never." I knew there would be times when my knee would make me want to surrender, but I could not. In John Cafferty's "Hearts on Fire" the lyrics state, "The cave that holds you captive has no doors, burnin' with determination to even up the score." I knew that I needed to use every ounce of determination to get through the pain. My favorite song from the soundtrack was Touch's "The Sweetest Victory," which says, "Hate and pain filled me up, every minute takes longer and longer, I bead of sweat 'cause drops of blood, make me stronger and stronger." I knew that overcoming the struggles would make me stronger.

I had Rocky's quote from the movie still in my head, and I worked out harder than ever. I did leg exercises such as leg curls, leg extensions, leg presses, hyperextensions and even squatted over 500 pounds with a torn ACL. For leg press, my dad had my 2 younger brothers sit on the machine and I had to press them up with my legs. He also held my feet over the attic opening and had me do 100 sit-ups. After that I used my weighted chop fit axe and did 100 ab chops. If that was not enough, my dad drove me to an enormous hill behind my grandmother's house and attached a 25-pound sled on my back. He had me run ten times up the hill. I put on the Nickelback's rocker "Follow You Home" and ran up that hill as hard as possible. My strength and determination were the best that they had ever been. I knew I still had much more hard work ahead of me, but I had the faith, hope, strength, and determination not to give up. No matter what, I could never give up.

That night, I dreamed I was pushing the Stone of Sisyphus back up the mountain. But this time, I had Steph and my father helping me push it up, and on the other side of the stone were Allison, Shane Hitt, Coach Smith, and Dr. Horton. They dug their feet and did everything to push the stone back down, but we would not let it happen. We used strength and determination to push it back up to the top. I woke in the middle of the night and needed to think about things. I went to my library in my room, pulled a book from it, and opened a secret passageway. Through the passageway were steps leading up to a tower at the top of my house. I was a huge Addams Family fan, so my PopPop next door designed this awesome secret passageway for me to access my private tower.

I had the attic room, so my secret tower is where I loved to sit, look at the stars, and reflect. I put on Chicago's power ballad "What Kind of Man Would I Be" and just thought about my life.

The lyrics of the song were, "Girl, well, it's been one of those days again, and it seems like the harder I try, over and over, I'm right back where I began, but you understand, oh girl." These lyrics genuinely related to my life because each time that I tried harder, I kept getting bad news just like Sisyphus who had to start over and over. Luckily, I had Steph, who always made me feel better. I knew I would not be the man I was without my girlfriend, father, and family. I knew that with the help of Steph and my family, I could push any stones back up any size hill. I just needed to find a way of telling Steph about my secret torn ACL...

CHAPTER 6: MOONLIGHT SERENADE

Within a short time, things went from horrible to wonderful for me. First, I found out that I tore my ACL, and the girl who I had a crush on for 3 years turned me down for the biggest jerk in the school. Then suddenly, I had the most amazing girlfriend I had been dating for almost a month, and my workouts were going incredibly. I had so much confidence and happiness in my life at that time. I was truly like Sisyphus because the stone kept rolling up and down for me. But at that moment, I was at the top and enjoying every ounce of it.

Steph made my life much more enjoyable because I knew I had someone other than my family who had my back. The only problem was that I still hadn't told her that I loved her yet or about my secret torn ACL. I loved her more than anything, but I wanted to tell her specially at a place called Kuser Park.

Kuser Park was a very private park in our town, behind the high school my mother attended. It had a really pretty gazebo and an old mansion built in 1892. Not many people went to the park, so it was very romantic. It was the park that inspired my very creative way of telling Steph that I loved her.

It was a beautiful spring day, and I took the tops and doors off my brand-new silver Jeep Wrangler, that my dad bought me for my 18th birthday. I drove her for about 5 minutes while we were blasting Chicago love songs such as "Call on Me" and "Love Me Tomorrow." I truly felt the lyrics of "Call on Me." "The feeling was clear, clear as the blue sky on a sunny day; everything was you." I asked her if she would close her eyes and not open them until I said to. She said yes but was a little confused.

I ensured she kept her eyes closed when we got to the park. I got my portable speaker out and turned on Chicago's "Will you still love me?" That was the first Chicago song I ever played for her when our eyes met at school. I then grabbed her hand and walked her slowly across the park. The wind blew her gorgeous, dirty blonde hair, and chills were forming all over my body. My eyes started to tear up as we glided through the park. It felt like a scene from a romantic movie as the song lyrics stated, "Til there was you, you and me, then it all came clear so suddenly, how close to you that I wanna be."

I then sat her down in the gazebo that I had decorated with roses and hearts.

"Open your eyes, sweetheart," I told her.

She opened her eyes and was ecstatic to see what I had done. I had decorated the gazebo like a picnic, and it had her favorite fruit and juice. I sat down next to her and looked into her beautiful brown eyes.

"Steph Marino. You make me so very happy; you make me the luckiest man on earth. Oh, my darling, I can't imagine my life without you. You lift me up when I'm feeling blue. All these years, I've searched, and now I found my missing piece, and it was you."

I quoted the new song I wrote for her, "It Was You." She looked at me with an enormous smile and happy tears dripping down her face. She was lost for words and did not know what to say. I pulled out my laptop computer and pressed play on a video I made for her. It was a music video of me driving my jeep mixed with pictures of Steph, symbolizing that she was all I thought about. It had the song "You Paint the Sky" by Chicago's Jason Scheff playing in the background. I was so emotional playing it for her, and she was so emotional watching it. Jason Scheff sang the lyrics, "You paint the colors I've never shown, you walk the mile I've walked alone, you show me truth that I've never known inside, you are the wings as I learn to fly, you are the morning instead of night, you're no illusion within my eyes, you paint the sky." The video finally was near the end, and I wrote, "I love you, Stephanie, You Paint the Sky" on the last picture in the clouds.

I then said, "Steph Marino, I love you. I love you so much!"

"That was... absolutely beautiful, Drew. I love you so much, too," she said and then kissed me directly on the lips.

We stayed in the gazebo for hours until it got dark, just cuddling, kissing, dancing, and listening to romantic love songs. We ate the fruit I bought her and dipped it in the sweetest whipped cream. It was one of the best and most memorable moments of my life, but I knew there was one more very important thing I needed to do.

Peter Cetera's song from *The Karate Kid Part II*, "Glory of Love," was playing. Right after my favorite part, when Cetera sings, "It's like a knight in shining armor, from a long time ago, just in time I will save the day, take you to my castle far away," I stopped the music.

"Steph, this has been one of the best days of my life. It has been like a wonderful fairy tale, but there is something really important that I need to tell you. I have been keeping a secret from you. I hated doing it, but this is extremely important. I know that I can trust you with it. You have to promise that you can never tell anyone. Not even your parents. Can you make that promise?"

She looked stunned and agreed. I felt like Peter Parker did for a second when he wanted to tell Mary Jane that he was Spiderman.

I hesitated momentarily but started to tell her, "So you know how I hurt my knee a few months ago, how I wear a brace, and how I told everyone that it's just a minor sprain?"

"Yeah," she replied nervously and confused.

"Well, I did hurt my knee. But, um....it's a lot worse than I've been telling people. I actually have a torn ACL in my knee. It requires knee surgery, but if I got the surgery now, I would have to miss my senior football season. So, although the Doctor said that there is a zero percent chance that anyone can play football with a torn ACL, I've decided to get a brace and try my absolute best to prove him wrong. I can't tell anyone because if the Coaches found out, they would never play me. If the other teams found out, they would try to injure me more. It's risky playing with this injury, but it's something I need to do. My knee feels fine now and I've been working out harder than ever with my dad to try and make it even stronger. I have faith that I can do this," I told her.

It took her a while before she finally said anything.

"Oh my gosh," she whispered. "You are so...brave and strong. I am so proud of you. I will be here for you every step of the way. I know that you can prove the Doctor wrong. I love you so much, Drew. So much..."

We kissed again, and I put on some more romantic songs. It started to get dark, so I lit the candles on the gazebo's sides. I took her hand, and we slowly danced under the moonlight with a sea of candles in the dark to Chicago's version of "Moonlight Serenade." Then all of a sudden it started to downpour, and the rain was shooting down the sides of the gazebo as we were dancing. It was so refreshing and beautiful. Celine Dion's gorgeous song "A New Day Has Come" played next, and as Celine sang, "Let the rain come down and wash away my tears, let it fill my soul and drown my fears, let it shatter the walls for a new sun," I could feel the rain washing away all my fears. I knew that a new day had come for me and Steph—a day filled with love and hope.

We thought it would be even more romantic to go out in the rain, so we stepped out of the gazebo and continued to dance and kiss in the pouring rain while listening to Celine's beautiful song. As we danced, I thought about all my fantastic times with Steph, like how our eyes met when we reached down to get my gym bag and our first kiss on her couch. It felt like a new day had come, and we would be in love for the rest of our lives. I got chills all over my body from how much I was in love and how cold I was from the rain.

The next song that played was the beautiful Peter Cetera and Chaka Khan duet "Feels Like Heaven," and at that moment, it truly felt like a heavenly fairy tale. As amazing of a night it was, I knew that my fairy tale could not last forever because the next morning started my morning football season workouts, and I would have to do everything with a completely torn ACL.

CHAPTER 7: FEELIN' STRONGER EVERY DAY

The following day, I had to wake up early for Coach McDuff's 6:00 am workout. It was late May, and the workouts would last until the start of football camp in August. Unfortunately, Coach McDuff was on vacation, so Coach Smith took over as the trainer.

Smith was in an extra grumpy mood, making us do bear crawls on the ground. They were tough on my injured knee, but I fought through the pain. Then he made us do sprints, and I could still outrun the entire team, even with my gigantic metal knee brace and torn ACL.

After our run, Coach Smith gave us our annual bench press test. Shane Hitt was still annoyed that I out-lifted him the year before and wanted revenge. Hitt went first, benching an impressive 15 reps at 185 pounds. I had the second-highest the year prior with 13 reps. I was nervous because Hitt outweighed me by about 40 pounds and looked confident, probably thinking there was no chance I could match or beat his repetitions. Coach Smith also had a cocky smirk on his face as he yelled at me to go next.

My dad was my spotter and got behind the bar to help me. This was an intense rivalry between two trainers and two athletes. In my head, I kept thinking about the Stone of Sisyphus, Rocky, Steph, Frankie's inspiring words, and the Doctor telling me it was impossible to play with a torn ACL. All those thoughts fueled my fire and inspired me to give everything I had on the bench press.

My dad whispered, "You got this, Drew. Let's wipe that obnoxious smirk off their faces."

My dad helped with the lift-off, and I pressed up each rep like it was a piece of cake. The first ten were easier than ever, but I started to struggle at 14 and could barely get it up. I needed one more rep to tie Hitt and two to beat him. Using every ounce of strength that I had, I finished the 14th rep. I got nervous because I still needed one more rep to tie Hitt and two to beat him. I used every ounce of strength I had to finish the 14th rep. I brought the 15th one down to my chest. At first, I was ready to give up until I thought about my nightmare of Hitt, Allison, Coach Smith, and Dr. Horton pushing the stone down on me.

I kept imagining that the bar was the stone and used all my force to manage somehow to get the 15th repetition up to tie Hitt. Hitt was stunned, and my dad wanted me to give up because he didn't think I could get the 16th rep. Still, I kept going. Tired of letting things bring me down, I did not want my nightmares to come true. I brought it down and thought about Hitt and Coach Smith yelling at me. I almost had it up, but then it slowly came back down on me. I still did not give up. Determined and with extra strength, I somehow pushed up the 16th rep to beat Hitt. Hitt, Smith, the team, and even my father were stunned. They couldn't believe that at 175 pounds, I bench-pressed 185 pounds 16 times. Hitt walked away ashamed, and Smith called the next guy up. He didn't even have the decency to tell me I did a good job or congratulate me.

Despite putting up with Smith and Hitt's garbage all summer, I still excelled in the morning workouts. We had to run sand sprints, and I would win every race. I refused to lose, even if I was in pain a lot of the time.

My summer went well, and we took day trips to my grandmother's beach house in Long Beach Island. Steph and I swam, worked out together, sunbathed, and shared peaceful moments in the gazebo at Kuser Park. Steph and I also went to the movies with Frankie Rossi and a few underprivileged children to give back to the community. We did a lot of community service and volunteer work. It was one of the best summers that I had ever had. The greatest moment was when I went to Las Vegas with Steph and my family in June. We went on vacation and to a Chicago the band concert and convention.

Steph had become a huge Chicago fan, too, and it was her first time seeing them live in concert, so she was excited. I also did something amazing and became friends with my all-time favorite singer, Jason Scheff, Chicago's tenor vocalist and bass player for 30 years. Scheff replaced Peter Cetera in the band after Cetera left for a solo career. Scheff was so impressed with my workouts and fitness pictures on social media that he gave me his cell number and wanted to exercise with me in Vegas.

The first time I talked to him on the phone was incredible. This was the guy I grew up listening to, and his posters were on my wall. I idolized him and couldn't believe I was talking to him on the phone. I told him about my football career, how much I loved his music and all the workouts I did with my father. He was so impressed that he agreed to work out with Steph and me in Vegas.

When we got to Vegas, Steph was amazed by how beautiful it was, especially the hotel we stayed at. My family always stayed at the Excalibur, a massive castle hotel. We had a fun-filled first night exploring Vegas-themed hotels like Paris, New York New York, Caesar's Palace, the Venetian, the Luxor, and many more.

The following day, we met Jason Scheff to work out. It was my second time meeting him in person and Steph's first. All three of us had an unbelievable hour workout together. Luckily, my dad could videotape and photograph us working out with our favorite singer. It was a dream come true, and we were in awe. We showed him some workouts, and he showed us some of his. We even shot a workout video set to Jason's inspirational song "Here I Am." Jason's song lyrics really resonated with me playing with a torn ACL. "To risk it all, fly or fall, I'm all in, cause it feels more right than any night I've ever lived; here I am, I'm holding my heart in my hands, I'm giving everything I have, I've had enough of holding back, I'm diving in now, here I go, I'm scared, and I can barely breathe but, fear won't get the best of me, nothing can make me miss this chance."

After the inspirational workout, it was time for the Chicago concert that night. Jason gave us front-row seats, and it was the best concert ever. I finally enjoyed their gorgeous love songs with the girl I loved sitting beside me. Jason was right in front of us, singing and playing bass, running around the stage. It was so cool seeing the guy we worked out with up on stage in front of thousands of people. Chicago is also the most diverse band ever so they played all of their different genres. They played almost every hit, such as "Make Me Smile," Old Days," Saturday in the Park," "Colour My World," ("I've Been) Searchin' So Long," "Feelin' Stronger Every Day," "Beginnings," and many others.

In the second verse of "Beginnings," Chicago founding member Robert Lamm sang, "When I kiss you, I feel a thousand different feelings, the color of chills all over my body." Steph and I kissed, feeling chills all over our bodies. At the song's end, founding members Lee Loughnane and Jimmy Pankow played their trumpet and trombone solos right in front of us and gave us a thumbs-up. They then played an acoustic set, and Jason came out and switched to the keyboard. On the keyboard, he sang my all-time favorite song, "Will You Still Love Me?" It was just Jason singing and playing, and it felt like he was singing it just for us.

When Jason sang "Will you Still Love Me," I had my arm around Steph. I pictured all the wonderful times we shared, replaying our first kiss, dancing in the gazebo, showing her the video, and many other moments. I kissed her, never wanting the moment to end. Steph's favorite moment came during the drum and percussion solo in the middle of the rocker "I'm a Man." More romantic moments came when the band got out their cellphones and had the crowd wave their phone lights during their number 1 1982 love song, "Hard To Say I'm Sorry."

The concert ended with a rocking version of the classic rocker, "25 or 6 to 4." It brought the house down and rocked extra hard. Afterwards, we got to go backstage to meet and take pictures with the rest of the band. It was truly one of my life's most remarkable and memorable nights.

We had more fun together during the rest of our time in Vegas. We loved swimming in the pool and sunbathing. We walked the Vegas strip and saw the Atlantis statue show at Caesar's Palace, the manmade volcano show at the Mirage, and many other shows. Our most romantic moment was when we went on the gondola boat ride in the Venetian hotel. It was so beautiful sitting next to the love of my life on the boat with my arm around her, listening to the Italian opera singer serenading us while looking at the sights of the exquisite Venetian hotel.

On the last night of the trip, our parents went to gamble, and my brothers were asleep. We had just returned from the gondola ride, and it was around midnight. We took the elevator up and decided to go to bed because it was so late. Our rooms were right next to each other, but as I opened the door to my room, I heard The Police's "Every Breath You Take" randomly start to play. Steph heard it too, and paused in her tracks. It was one of our favorite songs, and as Sting started to sing, "Oh can't you see you belong to me," we both turned around and looked into each other's eyes. We slowly walked towards each other, kissed, and she opened up her room door.

We both went in and kissed and cuddled in her bed. We held each other so tight and told each other how lucky we were to have one another. Steph eventually fell asleep in my arms. We both were devout Catholics, so we promised that we would not make love until marriage. I slowly removed the arm around her head and placed her head on the pillow. I tucked her in, kissed her on the cheek, then turned off the lights and entered my room.

Our vacation ended the next day. We all had tears in our eyes as we got on the plane because we did not want our fun to end. We felt like it was paradise there, but we knew we had to return to reality. On the plane ride home, Steph fell asleep on my shoulder, but I was too nervous to sleep. I was concerned about the upcoming season because I knew that I was going to have to give everything I had to get through it. I knew there would be times when I would fall, but I would have to do everything possible to stand back up.

CHAPTER 8: IF YOU LEAVE ME NOW

When we returned to New Jersey, Steph found a job as a cashier at a grocery store called ShopRite, and I hit the weight room harder than ever with my dad. My knee was feeling great, and I had hardly any pain. However, my pain-free days would soon end when my dad went to Italy with my mom for their 25th wedding anniversary in early July. My dad was concerned about leaving me alone with my injury, and while I shared his sentiments, I did not want to ruin his vacation with my mom.

They called us on the first day in Italy, expressing how beautiful it was and sharing their fantastic experiences. Meanwhile, I enjoyed some romantic alone time with Steph at home. We loved going through my secret passageway and sharing private time in my bedroom tower, looking at the stars while listening to beautiful love songs.

However, on their second day in Italy, I had a 7-on-7 football game in Pennsylvania. Coach McDuff had to drive me there because he knew I did not know the location. My relationship with Coach McDuff was the opposite of that with Coach Smith. We were close, and he respected me as a person and an athlete. Though he could be odd at times, I respected him too.

When Coach McDuff picked me up, a random guy named Tony with a ponytail was in the front seat. Coach McDuff introduced him casually, and in my head, I nicknamed him Tony Ponytail. I never discovered who he was, but I knew he was not a new coach. Despite the awkwardness, the car ride turned out to be fun, with McDuff and Tony Ponytail singing along to oldie music. When "She's Gone" by Hall & Oates came on, they belted it out. It was hilarious to hear McDuff and Tony Ponytail singing the songs, though they were horrific singers like my dad. They were no Hall and Oates, but it was cool to see a different side of the Coach that was not just football.

Coach McDuff, a retired cop dedicated to football, had never married. At 65, he had been coaching at St. Andrews for 20 years, hoping for a state championship in the upcoming season. I wanted more than ever to help Coach McDuff achieve his goal of winning a State Championship.

We finally got to the game, and I knew it would be the first ever football event that my father had not attended. He called me earlier to wish me luck, but that was not enough for me. I loved seeing his face on the sidelines or in the booth, but he was in another country. I put my brace on exactly how my father taught me, and I started the game on fire. I lined up as both running back and slot receiver. I had four catches and a touchdown within the first 7 minutes of the game. It was an incredible start to the season, and with the brace, I would have no problem proving Dr. Horton wrong.

But my high hopes went down the tubes on the next play. When I went to run a post-corner pattern, my knee buckled again, and I fell to the turf in agony. A post-corner pattern is when the receiver runs about 10 yards and then makes a cut inside as if he is going to run a post but then runs to the outside straight to the corner.

So, as I was making the sharp cut, the brace was not protecting my knee, causing it to twist. I fell to the ground in pain and thought that it was going to be a repeat of what happened to me in March. I could feel the stone pushing me to the bottom. I realized that sweat caused my brace to slide down because I was sweating so much. Therefore, the brace did not cover my knee or give it the support it needed.

The whole field became dead silent as I stayed on the ground for a moment to process what had happened. I knew I had to stand back up so I slowly got back on my feet. I was limping terribly, and Coach McDuff hurried over to help me. He asked if I was okay, and I gave him a painful smile and said, "Yeah, I just have to sit out the rest of the game and rest it."

The other team, Barton's athletic trainer, got me ice, so I sat there icing my knee while watching my team get their butts handed to them the rest of the game.

I sat there with so many questions in my head. "Was Dr. Horton right? Did I damage my knee even more? Is my football season over? Is my football career over? Will I ever be able to run again? Should I tell my dad and ruin his vacation?"

The game was over, and Barton beat us by about five touchdowns. Coach McDuff said that without me, the team lost its speed and momentum. He told me to rest the knee so that it would get better, but he had no idea the extent of the injury.

On the drive home, Tony Ponytail attempted to sing Chicago's number 1 1976 hit "If You Leave Me Now." The song made me think about how much I missed my dad. Eventually, Coach McDuff and Tony Ponytail dropped me off at home. It was the last time I ever saw or heard about Tony Ponytail, but I'll never forget him singing in the car and wondering who he was and why he was there.

I then called my father right away to tell him what had happened. I thought about waiting until he got home to tell him because I did not want to ruin his trip, but I knew that he would be mad at me if I waited. When I told him, he was so devastated that he wanted to come home right away to take care of me. But he still had three more days left, and I told him I would ice it down and it would improve.

He apologized and felt responsible, but I said it was nobody's fault. I said that the sweat caused the brace to slide down. My dad assured me he would find a way to prevent that from happening again. He also told me to go to my grandmother's house and soak my knee in the hot tub. I told him I would and not to worry about me and enjoy the rest of his trip.

Steph came over after her work and cheered me up. I had lost range of motion in my knee, and it was extremely swollen, so Steph drove me to my grandmother's house, and we used her hot tub. She was at her shore house, so we had the hot tub to ourselves. It made my knee feel better, and Steph and I also did our share of cuddling in the hot tub.

After we got out, my knee felt a little better, but I still was not 100 percent. I slept with my leg elevated on my couch for a few days. Each day, I woke up from the same nightmare of trying to push the stone up the hill, but every time I got close to the top, my knee buckled, and I fell. The one night was the worst because as I was falling, Tony Ponytail was singing his terrible version of "If You Leave Me Now." I woke up needing my dad's help. Then the alarm on my phone started to play, which was Chicago's song "Wake Up Sunshine." I remembered my dad singing that so badly to me as a baby. I realized that my dad was the sunshine that brightened my days for me, and I couldn't wait for him to come home. My knee was still sore, so I limped into the kitchen and put on Chicago's gorgeous orchestral piece, "Once Upon a Time," ironically the song I listened to when I first tore my ACL in the spring. It was a sad piece, making me miss my father even more. While listening to that and "Philadelphia morning" from *Rocky*, I did my daily Rocky routine of drinking raw eggs. It was horrible at first, but after doing it for years, I became used to it.

My dad finally came home from Italy to find me depressed because my knee was still swollen. He gave my brothers and me the souvenirs he got us in Italy and showed us many pictures from the trip. He could see that I was still upset, so he called me to his room for one of his inspirational chats. After every game or whenever I needed advice, he would call me to his room and always say something to cheer me up. But that time was extra hard to boost my morale.

When we were in his room, he sighed. "Drew, I'm so sorry I let you down. I should never have gone to Italy, but you can overcome this. I know you can. It sucks that you tore your ACL, but rough things are going to happen in life. Have you ever heard of the Greek Myth, the Stone of Sisyphus, like the Chicago song?"

I thought back to History class and the nightmares I had been having. I huffed. "Yeah, I know about Sisyphus. What's your point?" I asked sarcastically.

"My point is that life is like the Stone of Sisyphus. Sisyphus was cursed to roll a stone up a huge hill for eternity, but every time he reached the top of the hill, the stone would roll back down. That forced him to roll it back up again. Everyone's life is like Sisyphus' because we are all basically cursed to roll a stone. Life is a series of ups and downs; no matter how rich or famous you are, everyone's stone rolls down at some point. No one is on top of the hill their entire life. No one! However, what separates the winners and losers is that the winners are the ones who overcome their falls the most. Winners keep the stone from pushing them down the hill. They keep fighting to push it back, and if it rolls back down, they push it back again. You are a winner. I know you are. With this injury, there will be days when you're on top and days when you're way at the bottom. And right now, your stone fell. But it's time to push that stone back up. You have your family and Steph by your side. Roll that stone back up."

Once again, his speech tremendously boosted my mood. I hugged him so tight and told him that I loved him. My nightmares made more sense. In my dreams, I compared myself to Sisyphus, and every time something bad happened to me; the stone would roll down. My dad was right because I had to push the stone back up.

So I went up in my attic with my dad, blasted Boston's "More Than a Feeling" and Kansas' "Carry On Wayward Son" and did an all-upper body workout. I did so many biceps, triceps, chest, shoulders, and back exercises, and when I was done, I felt poised to get back to the top. I knew that I had a long road ahead of me, but thanks to my dad, I knew that I could accomplish anything.

CHAPTER 9: MAN TO WOMAN

There was only one more week before training camp started, and during that week, we stayed at my Grandmom's beach house in Long Beach Island. Thankfully, we were there because I soaked my leg in the hot tub, and miraculously, the swelling went down. I regained my full range of motion. More than that, I had another fabulous week with Steph.

We spent many romantic nights cuddling in the hot tub, pool and relaxing on the balcony upstairs. One night, Steph and I were lying on the lounge chair on the balcony, gazing at the half-moon and the stars. It was so peaceful that Steph fell asleep on my shoulder. The moment was so surreal that it inspired me to write a song called "Beach House Balcony of Love."

"Beach House Balcony of Love"

Verse 1:

Stars in the sky

Sitting so high

On your beach house balcony in LBI

Your darling is there

You're holding her

Hands running through her dirty blonde hair

It's your alone time, and you have so many feelings to share

Chorus:

On your beach house balcony of love

You want to tell her that she is the girl you've always dreamed of

Loving, kissing, hugging, and caring for forever

You will always remember those romantic nights on your beach house balcony of love

Verse 2:

It's a little bit cool

You hug her so tight as you see the reflections from the swimming pool

You look at her

To your surprise

She kisses you

Chorus:

On your beach house balcony of love

You want to tell her that she is the girl you've always dreamed of

Loving, kissing, hugging, and caring for forever

You will always remember those romantic nights on your beach house balcony of love

Bridge:

Then you take her hand and start to dance

This is the night that you start your eternal romance

Chorus:

On your beach house balcony of love

You want to tell her that she is the girl you've always dreamed of

Loving, kissing, hugging, and caring for forever

You will always remember those romantic nights on your beach house balcony of love

CHAPTER 10: NIGHT AND DAY

I felt a sense of pride in the song I had written, inspired by my beautiful girlfriend sleeping on the balcony. Chicago's beautiful rendition of "Night and Day" played softly in the background. Carefully, I lifted Steph and placed her in bed, giving her a goodnight kiss on the cheek.

The following morning, we both rose early to sit on the beach and witness the sunrise. Equipped with our cameras, in our bathing suits, and accompanied by a portable music speaker, we walked to the beach, just a block away from the house. It resembled a scene from a romantic movie as we sat, hand in hand, listening to the Righteous Brothers, precisely as the sun began to rise. As the song "Ebb Tide" played, a myriad of chills ran down my entire body as we shared a passionate kiss.

The sunrise was breathtaking, and Steph was captivated by its beauty. While I appreciated the sunrise, I was more enchanted by Steph's gaze as she marveled at it. It was amusing because she couldn't take her eyes off the sunrise, and I couldn't take my eyes off hers.

"Wow, so beautiful," I remarked.

"I know, isn't it," she replied.

"Oh, I'm not talking about the sunrise, silly. I'm talking about you. You're like a gift from—"

Before I could hear the end of her sentence, she kissed me on the lips. That moment inspired me to write another song titled "Her Eyes, Like the Sunrise."

"Her Eyes, Like the Sunrise"

Verse 1:

It's 4:00 am

Lying in bed

Holding your head

Unable to sleep

Then Stephanie turns to you

You turn on the light

Oh what a beautiful sight

As you stare and think

Chorus:

Her eyes are like staring at the sunrise

They shine so bright on a warm summer night

Her eyes have you mesmerized

Oh what a sight

Let's turn on the light

Go on the deck and watch the sunrise

But it's not as pretty as her eyes

Verse 2:

You have a nightmare, but wake up and stare at your angel lying there

You brush back her dirty blonde hair and think to yourself

Chorus:

Her eyes are like staring at the sunrise

They shine so bright on a warm summer night

Her eyes have you mesmerized

Oh what a sight

Let's turn on the light

Go on the deck and watch the sunrise

But it's not as pretty as her eyes

Bridge:

Take a walk on the beach with Stephanie

Walking through the sand

Holding her hand

You lay on the towel and say Wow

She's watching the sunrise

But you're just staring at her eyes

Chorus:

Her eyes are like staring at the sunrise

They shine so bright on a warm summer night

Her eyes have you mesmerized

Oh what a sight

Let's turn on the light

Go on the deck and watch the sunrise

But it's not as pretty as her eyes

After witnessing the sunrise, we took each other's hands and strolled into the ocean. The Righteous Brothers' "Ebb Tide" still played from my speaker. Submerged in the sea, we kissed, with the song and the gorgeous sunrise in the background. As we were kissing, a huge wave came up and hugged us. I wished someone had been there to capture that breathtaking moment. Unfortunately, my enchanted week in LBI had to end, and it was time for me to return to business and start training camp at St. Andrew's the following day.

CHAPTER 11: MORNING BLUES AGAIN

I returned to my hometown of Chambersburg, and my knee felt much better. My range of motion had returned all the way, and I was more ready than ever to play football. Even better news was that my dad came up with a great way to ensure my brace stayed on my leg at all times. He had the idea of using double-back Velcro and designed his connection to the brace. It helped keep the brace on my leg, even when sweating. I could not thank him enough.

My dad was the only one who knew how to execute his method correctly, and I could not trust the athletic trainer to keep my injury a secret. Many of my teammates would mock me when they saw my dad put on my knee brace, thinking I couldn't do anything without him. I didn't care if they made fun of me because they had no idea how severe my injury was.

When I went to camp on the first day, I learned about a few major changes. One significant change was that Shane Hitt had left our school and transferred to St. Greg's. He had gotten into trouble outside of school, and Coach McDuff threatened him to clean up his act or be benched. Although Hitt was our best defensive player, he was a huge cancer in the locker room. I actually thought it would be better for the team that he was gone, even though most of my teammates did not agree with me.

Tension was also building between Coach McDuff and Coach Smith because Smith blamed McDuff for pushing Hitt away. It was like two separate teams. Smith was the Defensive Coach and wanted to take his frustration out on McDuff's offense. McDuff wanted to do the same thing to Smith. The two sides essentially hated each other. Somehow, McDuff and Smith were able to work with each other for years, but their relationship was getting worse.

There was also a new 6-foot-2 recruited player named Tashawn Washington. There were rumors that they would use him to take over my running back position, especially if my knee hindered my performance. I was furious that these recruits would be treated like gods before they proved themselves. Fortunately, I got to take out my frustration and anger in our Oklahoma drill, which involved one offensive lineman, one defensive lineman, a linebacker, and a running back inside two small-spaced cones.

The goal of the drill was for the offensive lineman to block or push the defensive lineman a certain way to open ample space for the running back to run through. The defensive lineman's job was to avoid the offensive lineman and tackle the running back. The linebacker's job was to tackle the running back as well. My job as the running back was hitting the hole as fast as possible to get past the lineman and linebacker and score the touchdown. Each group got to go three times in the Oklahoma drill.

My first try did not go well because I got destroyed by both Tashawn Washington and the defensive lineman Bobby Benson. Coach Smith congratulated them, and I was crushed and saw colors, but my knee was still holding up. I was so embarrassed that I wanted to hide, but then I got flashbacks of my dad's Stone of Sisyphus speech and Dr. Horton telling me that it was impossible to play football with a torn ACL. I thought about pushing the stone back up the hill in my dreams and pictured kissing Steph at the Chicago concert.

Then, all of a sudden, I heard Steph's voice from the stands. She had come from work and surprised me. I didn't know she would be there that day, and she was why I managed to stand my ground and fight back. Steph even brought Frankie Rossi with her, and they were screaming, "Go Drew," from the bleachers. They inspired me so much that I was ready to stand get revenge in round 2.

On my second try, I got a nice block from my lineman. As Washington came charging in on my left side, I used my left arm and gave him a powerful, stiff arm to his helmet. It was such a strong, stiff arm that he fell to the ground, and I scored the touchdown. Steph, Frankie and my dad were cheering and clapping. Looking over at Steph and my dad being so proud of me gave me much happiness and confidence.

The Oklahoma drill was tied 1 to 1. I needed to win the next round to get back at Washington and Benson. I did not want to let Washington off with just a stiff arm. I had been on the team for four years, and he thought he could just come in as a freshman and be the team leader. No way. I needed to show him who the toughest person and leader of the team was. I wanted to run through him. I got down in my running back stance and looked straight ahead, anxiously awaiting Coach McDuff's whistle to start the drill. As soon as he blew it, I sensed Benson coming, so I did one of my famous spin moves and got past him. I then lowered my shoulder and ran right through Tashawn Washington so hard that he fell right to the grass. I flattened Washington like a pancake.

The whole team was stunned at first. Then they started cheering and clapping. Smith and Washington were furious, but my dad, Steph, and Frankie were ecstatic. I had proved that even with a torn ACL, I was still the strongest guy on the team. I gave Steph a wink through my helmet, and she winked back. I was so happy that I proved I could make it through the camp after one day with a torn ACL. Still, the rest of the camp would be even harder to overcome.

It was like a roller coaster ride full of ups and downs. We were doing double camp sessions. The first session was from 8 am to 11 am, and the second was from 2 pm to 5 pm. We had training camp every day except for Sundays, and participating in camp in the 95-degree weather with a cumbersome metal knee brace and a torn ACL wasn't easy at all. It was one of the hardest things that I ever had to do. It required a lot of mental toughness and a strong will to fight through the pain. It was almost a miracle how I got through the camp.

The most challenging week of camp came when I sprained my left ankle running a pass pattern. We practiced on an old baseball field, and one day, while running a pattern, I rolled my ankle on an old base hidden in the grass. I had a sprained ankle on my left foot and a torn ACL on my right knee, but I refused to sit out. I was in so much pain, but I just kept playing hard. About 30 minutes after I sprained my ankle, it was time for our team's first inner-squad scrimmage. I was nervous because it would be a battle between Coach McDuff's offense and Coach Smith's defense, but my ankle was hurting terribly. My dad quickly got some tape and taped my ankle around my spikes.

"Drew, I know you are in pain, but you have to fight through it. You can't sit out and let them get someone else to take your spot. Just get through this scrimmage and use everything you have. You got this," my dad said to me while taping my ankle.

It was time to start the scrimmage, and unfortunately, Coach McDuff called a play that I got the ball first on. It was going to be a pitch sweep to the outside. The quarterback would pitch me the ball, and I would run to the outside on my injured ankle. I was hoping that I would be able to run well despite the piercing pain.

The quarterback, Brady, shouted, "Hike!"

I exploded out of my stance. I felt so much pain in my ankle and knee but kept running as fast as possible. I put my arm out and stiff-armed the outside linebacker and the middle linebacker. Washington was coming towards me to tackle me. I saw him coming in the corner of my eye, and I spun around so quickly that he completely missed me and flew into the sidelines. The team was cheering, and I had no idea how I just did that with a torn ACL and sprained ankle. I had so much determination; it was one of my best scrimmages ever.

I ran for about 100 yards and scored two touchdowns, but I could not stop limping as soon as practice was over. It was crazy how I could go from running all over Coach Smith's defense one minute to hardly being able to walk the next. My teammates did not understand it either, but I told them that football made people do amazing and unexplainable things. I loved the game so much that it inspired me to give everything I had. I was determined to overcome any roadblock that was in my way. Although my body felt like garbage, my mind felt incredible that night. I was so proud of myself and knew that if I could get past that day, I could get past anything.

That night, I went swimming with Steph, and the water made my joints feel great and refreshed. Although I had a fantastic first day, and my ankle was healing, the rest of my training camp did not go very well. My line struggled very much, and I had no blocking or spaces to run through most of the time. Coach Smith's defense would tackle me in the backfield as soon as I got the ball because my linemen could not block well.

I kept my starting job as a running back, but my team passed 70 percent of the time. It was frustrating that Coach McDuff did not let me run the ball a lot, but I was used to it because McDuff loved to pass. Somehow, I was able to get through camp without missing one practice or scrimmage. I had my tremendous girlfriend Steph always to cheer me up whenever I was down and hurting. I was also lucky to have Steph, my brothers, my mother, and especially my father by my side. I didn't know what I would have done without their support. Although I made it through camp without injuring my knee more and was still the starting running back, my character would be tested even more in our first scrimmage against Williams High School.

CHAPTER 12: THE INNER STRUGGLES OF A MAN

Our scrimmage occurred about an hour from our school at the defending public school champions, Williams High School. It was a hot and challenging day, with the scorching turf making it even more difficult. The game started roughly for me as on my first three carries, I was tackled in the backfield as soon as I received the ball. The defenders swarmed in on me like ants converging on food particles. The Williams' defensive line tore our offensive line apart, and Coach McDuff screamed at our line to play more intensely. However, their defense proved too big and strong for our offense. I was getting beat up as soon as I received the handoffs, with no holes for me to run through.

Coach McDuff decided to pass more, and midway through the scrimmage, he instructed me to run a down-and-out pattern near the sidelines. This pattern was the same one I ran when I tore my ACL back in the spring. Unfortunately, this pattern brought terrible luck once again, as the strap on my knee brace came undone due to the sweat on the Velcro, causing it to disconnect. My knee buckled, and I fell to the ground in intense pain.

Furious, I blamed my father, who was filming the game up in the booth. My family and Steph came down to check on me. Despite knowing it wasn't my father's fault, I was so upset that I took it out on him.

My dad felt terrible and said that I would overcome it and that next time, he would tape it down so it would not disconnect again. My mother and Steph hugged me, but I was still distraught. My dad got me ice, and I had to sit on the sidelines for the rest of the scrimmage and watch my team get pulverized. I sat there thinking that this was the third time I fell that year, and in my mind, I thought it might be too much to overcome. I felt that my knee had to be damaged more, and I did not think that I had many more lives left in me.

I was devastated, but after the game, my parents took my brothers, Steph, and me out to eat at a nice restaurant. They made me feel much better and even made me laugh a little. My time out with my family was a great distraction, but I knew I had a lot to overcome before the start of the season.

My knee was pretty bad, and I only had two days to make it better before Monday's practice. There was only one more week before the first game of the season. So I kept icing it down, stayed off of it all weekend, and soaked it in my Grandmom's jacuzzi with Steph.

One night, I could not sleep, so I snuck out of my house, got in my car, and drove around while listening to "If It Were You" and "Come in From the Night" by Chicago. I just wanted to get some air and think about things, but then I passed by my church and thought that maybe I could go in and say a prayer. I didn't know if it would be open because it was so late at night, but I thought I would try. So I parked my car, got out, and was pleasantly surprised that the door was open.

There wasn't a soul in sight. I just sat in the first pew and prayed that God would heal me and people who were sick. I looked up and saw Jesus in front of me, on the cross. I thought about how tough He was. I remembered that Jesus fell three times, and He was in much more pain than I was, yet He overcame everything to save all of mankind. I just felt like a baby complaining about an injured knee when Jesus went through torture and died for us. His toughness and strength inspired me again to not give up.

That Monday, the swelling miraculously went away. Monday was also the start of my Senior school year, and I was hoping that it would be a great year in school, both in the classroom and on the football field.

CHAPTER 13: MANIPULATION

It was the first day of school that Monday and I was so excited to see that Steph was in my English class. The hard part was going to be paying attention to the teacher and not Steph's beauty, but I had pretty decent self-control with that stuff. Unfortunately, I found out that my ex-crush, Allison Hanson, was in another class of mine, History. I had not talked to her since the day she blew me off. It was very awkward because not only was she in my class, but she sat right in front of me.

When she first walked in, I got nervous to see her but then gave her a friendly hello. I followed Jesus' rule of turning the other cheek. She gave me a friendly smile back. She turned to the front, and we did not say another word to each other until the end of class. I could tell that there was tension between us and that she felt weird sitting in front of me.

To my surprise, she turned around at the end of class and said, "I can't wait to wear your number on my cheek this Saturday."

My jaw dropped. I had completely forgotten that I told her that she could wear my number the previous school year before I started dating Steph. I did not know what to say, so I just gave her a smirk as the bell rang to end the class. I was shocked that she still wanted to wear my number after she blew me off for Shane Hitt. I knew I had to tell Steph what was happening, but I needed to figure out how to do it without angering her.

When I left my History class, Thomas Simmons tracked me down to tell me about his exciting summer. He kept rambling on about some science camp that he went to and used words I could not even understand. I was friendly to him, as always, but I had more important things on my mind, like how to deal with Allison Hanson trying to wear my number on her cheek.

It was finally time for lunch, and I explained everything to Steph. She understood but wanted me to tell Allison she couldn't wear my number the next day. Steph and I had a great lunch together in the courtyard. At the end of the day, we had English together, and she ended up sitting right across from me. I had thought that I would not be distracted, but I was mesmerized by her gorgeous brown eyes.

When the bell rang, I walked her out to the bus and hugged and kissed her before she got on it. I had to go to football practice, and she was going home. I hated leaving her, even if it was only for two hours. I stood there and looked at her beautiful eyes, gazing at me through the bus window. As the bus pulled away I put on Chicago's classic love song "If You Leave Me Now" because hear leaving took away the biggest part of me. She gave me a wink and blew me a kiss. I did the same thing back, and I watched her until the bus pulled away from the school.

I then reported to football practice, and Coach McDuff gave us our brand-new football jerseys. They were so patriotic-looking being that our team name was the St. Andrew Americans. The home jersey was blue with white sleeves and a giant American flag in the middle of the sleeve. It also had two silver stripes going down the sides of the jerseys to match our silver pants. The silver pants had two giant blue and white stars on the sides. The away jersey was white with blue sleeves and an American flag in the middle of the sleeve, with two silver stripes going down the sides of the jersey. When Coach McDuff handed me my new jersey with my number 22, I was so excited to try it on. The number 22 had a lot of importance to me. My father wore that number, and he wore it because the first Italian Stallion before Rocky wore the number 22. His name was Johnny Musso, and he played college football at the University of Alabama. Sylvester Stallone also wore the number 22 when he played football so I proudly wore my favorite number.

After we got our new uniforms, we had film sessions

and were studying the film on the team we would play that Saturday. That team was called the Clarence Cardinals, one of our biggest rivals. Clarence was the team that snapped our 58-game winning streak two years before and had beaten us two years in a row since then.

As Coach Smith so eloquently put it, "They own us! They want to make it three years in a row! They want to pulverize you! They want to destroy you!"

Fortunately, Coach McDuff calmed him down. We started watching their film, and their defensive line was so huge that they tore the opposing running backs apart. In the back of my mind, I was terrified that they would do the same thing to me and make my knee even worse. My fear didn't stop the next day because I soon had to tell Allison she couldn't wear my number 22 on her cheek. I did not know if I was more afraid of the massive Clarence lineman or this popular cheerleader with a massive ego.

So a few minutes before history started, Allison and I were just in the room.

I said, "Allison, can I uh talk to you for a minute? I'm not sure if you know this, but Steph Marino and I are dating now. When you asked to wear my number on your cheek, it was before I was dating her. I'm sorry, but I don't think it would be right if you still wore my number."

I watched her big smile change into this surprised frown. She looked really upset and did not say anything.

I sighed. "I'm sorry Allison. I used to have the biggest crush on you. That's why I asked you to lunch last year. I thought you liked me back, but then you blew me off without even telling me and ended up going with Shane Hitt instead. You shattered my heart." I told her with an intense look on my face.

She took a deep breath. "I liked you too. I still like you. I made a mistake. The reason that I broke up with Shane was that I have feelings for you. Shane and I are done. I want to be with you now." She told me with tears in her eyes.

But I shook my head. "I'm sorry, but it's too late. I'm with Steph now, and I love her more than anything," I said.

"But I'm the Captain of the Cheerleading Squad and future homecoming queen," she said sarcastically.

"But Steph is the Captain of my heart. My heart belongs to her. I don't care how popular you are. I gave you a chance last year, and you blew it. You are only giving me attention now because Shane left. If Shane were still here, you'd want to wear his number. I love Steph. I'm sorry," I told her.

She got so upset that she stormed out of the classroom before the class even started, right as our teacher was walking in. The teacher looked confused and asked, "What happened with Allison?" I told her it was a long story, but she would be okay.

Allison came back for the start of class and would not even look at me. I felt terrible, but it was all true. She broke my heart and wanted to date me after things with Shane Hitt blew up in her face. I knew that she would still be with him if Shane had never left.

Later, I told Steph everything, and she gave me a tremendous hug. She looked worried about Allison trying to take me away from her, but I assured her she did not have to worry. I told her that she was the only one I wanted. She hugged me again and kissed me right on the lips.

That Friday night, Steph and I went to the movies. Ironically, as we were in line buying our popcorn, we ran into Allison and Shane Hitt. She must have started dating him again after I told her she could no longer wear my number.

Hitt saw me and screamed, "Russo, after Clarence destroys you, we will next week! I'm going to bury you alive! And you might want to get some extra protection on your bum knee!"

I wanted to punch him in the face so badly but I knew that I just needed to wait until the next week to get my revenge on him during the game. I still kept my cool and tried to turn the other cheek. I used legal forms of revenge like sports to get back at people.

I tilted my head slightly toward him and said, "Thanks for the kind words, Shane. See you next week."

I then took Steph's hand and walked away. Hitt laughed and called me a coward as I walked towards the theatre. Then he called me a chicken, which reminded me of a scene from *Back to the Future*. So, like Marty, when he learned from his mistakes and ignored Needles in *Back to the Future Part III*, I ignored Shane Hit and just kept walking away.

As we walked away, Steph got worried. "He is going to try to take your knee out next week. You can't play."

"Steph, don't worry. I'm not going to let him hurt me. I promise," I said as I put my arm around her.

We sat in our seats in the theatre, and the lights went dim. We kissed right before the start of the movie. In the back of my mind, I was scared to death about Hitt trying to hurt me, but that kiss from Steph made me feel much better.

Meanwhile, Allison was furious with Shane. It was so awkward because as we were walking away, I heard some of their conversation.

"You are such a jerk! Drew is such a better man and football player than you!" Allison screamed at him.

Hitt was furious, and Allison broke up with him again. She was afraid to go outside alone with him so she went into the theatre to find me. She sat next to me and whispered in my ear what had happened. She told me that she was afraid to be outside alone with him, so she asked if she could sit with me and if I could drive her home. I told her she could, but I also told Steph what had happened. She was not happy but knew it had to be done for Allison's safety.

It was so awkward because I was sitting between my girlfriend and my old crush, who broke my heart. I could see them giving each other dirty looks in the corner of my eye. It even got more awkward because Thomas Simmons somehow came walking into the theatre and sat right next to Allison. He said, in a loud, obnoxious voice, that he saw Steph's status on my Facebook that said we were going to the movies.

"You guys must have forgotten to invite me," he yelled.

Everyone in the theatre then told him to be quiet. Steph whispered to me that she would not post Facebook statuses anymore. I agreed and laughed. Thomas sat next to Allison, and she looked so grossed out by him. Eventually, Allison fell asleep during the movie and leaned her head on Thomas' shoulder. Thomas was so excited that he was drooling all over her.

When the movie ended and Allison woke up, she was shocked and terrified to wake up in Thomas' arms.

She quickly got away from him and said, "Ew. Was the ceiling leaking or something? My hair is wet."

Steph and I told her it might have been and chuckled because we knew it was drool from Thomas.

We all walked out of the theatre together when Shane Hitt came out of his car.

He growled menacingly at our group before turning to Allison. "So Allison, you ran to your hero, Russo, to protect you? Doesn't he have a girlfriend? Or are you dating the dork? This is the biggest group of losers I have ever seen. Let's see who the real man is Russo. Let's settle this now. Fight me!" he screamed.

I shook my head no. "We'll settle this next week on the field," I said before calmly walking away.

He was furious, and I knew he would be fueled up to play me the following week. I asked Thomas if he could take Allison home. He agreed right away, but Allison was surprised.

"What? I thought you were gonna drive me home Drew," she said annoyed.

"Thomas lives much closer to you. Have fun, guys," I said.

When they were a distance away, I turned to Steph. "Hopefully, Thomas will keep his eyes on the road, not Allison." She laughed.

When we got to Steph's house, "REO Speedwagon's "Can't Fight This Feeling" played in my car. I gave her a long, good night kiss, even though I wanted to go inside and cuddle on the couch with her. I knew I had to get up extra early for our first game the next morning, so I drove home blasting one of my favorite pump-up songs, "Separate Ways" by Journey. I was so furious with Hitt that I would use it as motivation for the Clarence game the following day. I was more ready than ever for the opening game of the season against the Clarence Cardinals.

CHAPTER 14: BEGINNINGS

That morning, Chicago's rocker "25 or 6 to 4" blasting from my alarm woke me up, and I knew that it was game day. I woke up and took a hot shower while listening to the song from the *Rocky IV* soundtrack, "The Sweetest Victory. I hoped the day would end with a sweet victory. I eventually got to my school and had to hear the obnoxious rap music that my team was blasting in the locker room. The rap music made me nervous, so I put on my headphones and listened to more of the *Rocky IV* soundtrack to drown out the sound of the rap music and Coach Smith screaming at his defense.

I then got my football equipment on and my dad came and put my brace on me with his Velcro method. He taped it extremely tight so that it would not come off. My knee felt so much better and I was ready for the game. We headed on the bus to Clarence's field, which was right down the road.

It was eventually game time, and our team won the coin toss, which meant we would receive the ball first. I was the kickoff returner and I was standing back there anxiously anticipating to catch the kickoff so that I could run it back for a touchdown. The marching band's drums started to play, and I could see the opposing team lined up at the other end of the field, getting ready to come down and attack us. It felt like a war scene in those ancient warrior movies and both teams were standing on opposite ends getting ready to go to battle. The whistle finally blew, and the start of my Senior football season was underway.

The ball was kicked, and I felt like everything was in slow motion. It was kicked right to me but bounced first on the ground. I quickly scooped the ball up and ran as fast as I could. I then saw the first Clarence Cardinal approaching, and I made a sharp cutback move to avoid him. Then another Cardinal came, so I did a spin move on him. After the spin, I was in the clear.

There was no Cardinal in sight; all I had to do was keep running straight, and I would be in the end zone.

I could hear all the fans cheering as I ran as fast as possible into the end zone for the touchdown. It was one of the best feelings in my life because I returned a kickoff for a touchdown on the first play of my Senior season. I could see my parents and Steph's proud faces. Steph and my mother were wearing my other 22 jerseys to support me.

Then, in a moment, my amazing feeling came crashing down faster than lightning. I found out that there was a flag on the play and that the touchdown was called back. My teammate committed a holding penalty because he grabbed the Cardinal player's shirt. It was like the Stone of Sisyphus again. As soon as I pushed the stone up to the top, it dropped back down within seconds.

Unfortunately, my low would last for the entire game. Coach McDuff kept trying to call pass plays, and our offense just could not get into any rhythm because we could hardly complete a pass or get any yardage. I finally got my first run of the game, and it was a disaster. I ran a play to the inside, but my right guard could not block their 300-pound defensive tackle. Their defensive tackle annihilated me as soon as I got the football into my hands. He knocked me back into the grass, and I was seeing colors. Chicago's song "Watching All the Colors in My Head" played in my head, but I could shake off the dizziness and slowly get back up.

The next play was a pass, and my job was to stay by the quarterback and try to protect him so that he could pass without getting sacked. Once again, our guard missed the 300-pound defensive lineman on the Cardinals and came right in to try to tackle the quarterback. I used every bit of strength and force and somehow pushed him back about two yards. I didn't let him tackle the quarterback, but unfortunately our quarterback, Andrew Brady threw an interception on that play.

The Cardinals' defensive back returned the interception 70 yards for a touchdown.

That play ended the first half, and they had a 21-0 lead at halftime. At halftime, Coach Smith and Coach McDuff were furious, and they screamed at us. They said that we did not show up to play, and they were 100 percent right, but they did not show up to coach either. Their plays were highly predictable, and Clarence could stop us on every play. My dad came to see if my knee was holding up. I told him that it was holding up but I was very disgusted with the game. He told me to keep my head up and to keep running hard.

We started strong in the second half and marched the ball into their red zone. We were on the 5-yard line and only needed five more yards to score a touchdown. They called my number for a pitch sweep play, and I was excited. I wanted to score my first touchdown of my Senior season so badly. Brady called hike, and our slot receiver, Mike Matthews, went in motion before the ball snapped to serve as my lead blocker. Matthew's job was to block the defensive end so I could get around him, but the chances are never very good when a 140-pound player has to block a 270-pound defensive end. It is like a sports car going head-to-head with a monster truck. Matthews missed the defensive end entirely, and he destroyed me as soon as I caught the pitch sweep.

Then Coach McDuff called a quarterback bootleg, which is when the quarterback fakes the handoff and runs around the end. Once again, the defensive end was not blocked, and he sacked Brady behind the line of scrimmage. The next play, they called a pitch sweep to me again, but this time it was to the other side of the field. This time, our 130-pound slot receiver, Steve Jenkins, was supposed to block their 260-pound defensive end. Once again, our slot missed the defensive end completely, and I was hit in the backfield as soon as I caught the pitch.

It was then 4th down, and I could hear the booing from

the stands. As I was on the ground underneath the massive lineman, all I could picture was the Stone of Sisyphus rolling back down. I could hear Dr. Horton saying it was impossible to play football with a torn ACL. I just wanted to lay there and go to sleep, even though it would have been a bit weird sleeping with a 260-pound defensive end on top of me. I knew I could not give up, so I got up for the next play, and Andrew Brady threw an incomplete pass. The Cardinals had stopped us from scoring a touchdown and gained the ball back.

They ended up shutting us out for the rest of the game and the final score was 27-0. We started the season 0 and 1. When the game was over, we walked to the bus like zombies. Our fans were dead silent and I left my helmet on until I got to the bus because I was too embarrassed to show my face.

As we walked off the field, I could see Steph standing with my parents. She looked so sad for me. We both locked eyes and shared a passionate moment just with our eyes. Then I turned and saw Allison walking out with the cheerleaders. I was shocked to see that she still had my number 22 painted on her face, even though I asked her not to. I had hoped Steph had not seen it because she would have flipped out if she did. It was annoying that she did that, but I would have to deal with it after. After our horrible loss, that was the least of my concerns.

After our bus returned to the school, I entered my parents' car. Steph gave me a big hug to try and cheer me up. The Chicago song "Heart in Pieces" was playing; ironically, my heart felt like it was in pieces.

When we got home, my dad put ice on my knee and I laid down with Steph on the couch in silence. I was so upset, and I knew that I had a long season ahead of me. That was only the beginning; I needed to overcome that terrible game and have a better season. Luckily, my knee was not in too much pain. It was just a little sore and needed to rest. I just needed to take my mind off the game, and Steph knew the best medicine for me.

CHAPTER 15: GETAWAY

Steph and I were sitting on the couch in silence. I still had tears remaining in my eyes. After about 10 minutes of sulking, Steph finally snapped. She got a tissue and wiped the tears off of my eyes.

"That's it. I'm tired of this. We are going out."

I was still depressed, but my dad said that was a great idea, so I went with her.

We got in her car, she put on Chicago's song "Now" and started to drive. The song was one of my favorites and it was very upbeat with a positive message. The song said, "Now this is the time we must start living in; let's make a change while it's not too late." I knew that I needed to focus on the here and now and not the past. I needed to forget the last game and move forward. It was already starting to cheer me up. Then she played some of my favorite Billy Joel songs like "Uptown Girl" and "Only the Good Die Young." I kept asking her where we were going, but she said it was a surprise. It took me about 20 minutes, and I realized she was taking me to Long Beach Island. She packed my bathing suit, and I did not even know it.

My Grandparents, Aunt, and Uncle were still at their summer house until October, so we went there to visit. My grandparents always cheered me up, and my grandfather told me funny jokes and teased me like always. My Grandmother offered us so much food, as always, with her sweet and high-pitched voice. She was a true Italian Grandmother who kept hounding us to eat until we stuffed our faces. It was almost impossible to go over to her house without eating something.

We swam in her pool, which felt great because my aching joints were still hurting from the game. Then my Grandmother gave us $50 and told us to use it at Fantasy Island, a park in Long Beach Island with carnival rides, food courts, shops, and games. We had a fantastic night on Fantasy Island with the money that my Grandmother had given us. We played some fun games and rode a few carnival rides.

After Fantasy Island, we returned to my Grandmom's house and cuddled on the chair outside on the balcony. We stayed there for a few minutes before I took a deep breath.

I turned to my girlfriend. "Steph, you are the greatest thing that ever happened to me. Before I met you, I was dead inside. I was so lonely, and all I would do was exercise all day, but now I am so happy with you. I can't imagine my life without you. I have been keeping a little secret, though. I don't know much about music, and I'm not good at singing at all, but I wrote you a few song melodies. I have also been secretly taking online singing lessons. I still need to improve, but I have gotten much better. Can I sing you a song called "Beach House Balcony of Love?"

She stared at me momentarily, then gave me a happy smile. "Aw. You are the most amazing boyfriend ever. Of course, you can."

I was very nervous, but I started singing it to her. "Stars in the sky, you're sitting so high, on your beach house balcony in L.B.I., your darling is there, you're holding her." I didn't sound great, but I tried. While I was singing, she was crying.

When I was done singing it, she had a huge smile on her face.

"That was the most beautiful thing ever. You were amazing. I love it."

I gave her a sheepish grin. "No, I'm not that great at all."

"You aren't a pro singer, but you just took lessons for me and sounded really good. I don't care if you aren't a pro singer. It came from your heart with so much passion and emotion. This moment will always be one of the most memorable moments of my life. When I thought that you couldn't get any more romantic, you do this. You are too incredible, Drew Russo," she said with so much conviction.

I was shocked that she loved it so much. "Thanks, but you're more amazing, Steph Marino. I wrote a few more songs, but I want to wait until I become a better singer for them and maybe get some instruments behind them."

While she wanted to hear them immediately, I kept reassuring her that she would, just as soon as I practiced a bit more.

Then all of a sudden, I heard a noise. I looked back and saw my Grandmom, Grandpop, Aunt, and Uncle running away from the window. They must have been spying on us when they heard me singing. I found it funny, even though they heard me sing. Steph and I were laughing, and then she kissed me right on the lips. We then started to slow dance on the balcony until we got tired. We went to bed, and when we woke up the next morning, we got up early to watch the sunrise on the beach.

It was an incredible morning, but I knew it was time to return to business. After we sand-sprinted on the beach, we went back to the house and gave my Grandparents, Aunt, and Uncle hugs and kisses goodbye. My family is Italian so we always hugged and kissed. I knew it was time to leave the fantasy world and get back to reality. Reality was ready for me, but would I be ready for reality?

CHAPTER 16: CRITICS' CHOICE

When we got back to my house, my dad was on the computer and was acting strange.

"What's going on?" I asked him.

"Don't worry about it," he said, annoyed.

"No, let me see," I told him angrily.

When I saw what he was looking at, I saw the fans bashing me online on the high school football blogs.

One person wrote, "Russo is a hard-working kid, but his injury has taken its toll on him."

Another person wrote, "Russo just doesn't have it this year. He needs to be benched."

My dad saw me almost cry and told me not to let it get to me. "Those guys are idiots hiding behind a computer and don't know what they are talking about. Don't worry about it, Drew," my dad told me, but it hurt so much.

That entire Sunday, I didn't even watch the NFL. I sat there with Steph and kept replaying the game film repeatedly. I kept watching, and I saw how poorly our team blocked. It was not my fault because most of the time, I was getting tackled as soon as I got the ball in my hands. I even listened to the sad Chicago song "Critics' Choice" because I was giving everything I had on the field, and it was not good enough for these critics.

That day, Chambersburg held their annual Feast of Lights and procession where all Italians would process down the streets in honor of "Our Lady of Casandrino," the patroness of the Italian town near Naples, where my ancestors were from. My grandparents next door would have all of our relatives come over to watch the procession from the porch. Then my

MomMom would make her homemade pasta, and we would all go and celebrate in her basement. After dinner, it was time for the Feast of Lights, a vast Italian carnival on the streets of Chambersburg. They had rides, incredible food, and excellent music, such as Frankie Valli and the Four Seasons, Johnny Maestro and The Brooklyn Bridge, Frank Sinatra, Dean Martin, and Chicago's classic song "Saturday in the Park." It was fun hanging out with Steph, Frankie, and my family at the feast.

I felt a lot better after being with family and friends. Still, that night, I had another nightmare about the entire Clarence defense: Shane Hitt, Dr. Horton, Tashawn Washington, and Allison, who had my number on her cheek. Once again, they were pushing the stone down on me. What was even scarier was Thomas Simmons, and his Latin club were on top of the hill, singing some spooky Latin chant. I woke up and screamed again. My parents came running in. I told them what had happened, and they said I would overcome everything. I wanted to believe it, but I wasn't sure if I could.

I took a hot shower to calm myself down and then drove to school. I knew it was time to deal with Allison. I had to get a little mean even though I was always respectful. However, she managed to find me before I could say anything.

"Your girlfriend told me to stop wearing my number," Allison said.

I was shocked because I didn't even know Steph saw her wear the number because she didn't mention it. Allison said she would stop wearing it, and to my surprise, she apologized. It almost seemed too easy because I expected a sarcastic or nasty comment from her.

After History class, Thomas Simmons found me and claimed that Allison had been texting him nonstop ever since that night at the movies. I found it hard to believe, but I did not say anything. I wanted to let him have his moment in the sun. I didn't think it was possible for someone like Allison to be interested in Thomas, but I had more important things to worry about.

At lunch, I thanked Steph for taking care of Allison and asked her why she didn't tell me she saw her wearing my number. She said I was already in an awful mood and didn't want to make me feel worse over something insignificant. I thanked her for being so supportive and sweet.

Then, all of a sudden, I noticed that a bunch of students were making fun of my stats in the paper from the Clarence game. The newspaper said that I had 6 carries for minus 16 yards. Being that I recovered a fumble in the backfield and landed on the ball, it counted as negative yards for me. Although it hurt my feelings, I could not dwell on the critics. I did know that things were just not going my way.

Things worsened at practice when I learned I would have to share my running back position with Tashawn Washington. Washington was Coach Smith's new favorite player, and they wanted to try him out at running back. I was angry, but I knew I would have to prove myself again. I went out to the practice field in shorts since I had to wait for my dad to finish teaching to put my knee brace on properly so it wouldn't slide down. He finally got there, and I told him the bad news. He was furious too, but he said that I had to go out and kick butt.

That practice was one of my best. Despite my torn ACL., I felt faster than ever. The metal knee brace slowed me down a bit, but I was still one of the fastest players on the team. We timed in the 40-yard dash again, and I still ran the fastest time, even with the knee brace and torn ACL.

Coach Smith was outraged.

"Come on, Washington! You can't let Russo beat you with a bum knee!" He screamed to him.

He made me race him 5 times, and all 5 times, I beat him.

I felt a lot better after practice, so I went to the movies with Steph that night. When we entered the theatre, we were shocked to see Thomas and Allison come and join us. It looked like they were out on a date.

When I approached them, I asked, "Are you guys dating?"

"No, we are just friends," Allison responded immediately.

I knew that something wasn't right, though. It seemed as if Allison was up to something. When Allison went to the bathroom, Thomas showed me his texts with Allison.

"Look how much Allison is texting me," he said excitedly.

I saw the texts, and almost all of them were about me. I realized that Allison was using Thomas to get closer to me. I knew I couldn't tell Thomas because it would've broken his heart. But I knew that I needed to do something to stop what was happening.

When Allison returned from the bathroom, I caught her staring at me during the movie. Steph caught her, too, and gave her a dirty look. I felt so bad that Thomas didn't notice her looking at me.

After the movie, I wanted to confront Allison privately, but we hit a roadblock. We ran into Shane Hitt, some snobby cheerleaders, and his boys from St. Greg's.

"Well, if it isn't Mr. 6 for -16 yards, boy, over there. You're going to go 6 for -60 tomorrow night. I'm going to put you in the E.R.," he threatened.

We ignored him, so he tried again. "Allison, are you going out with Mr. Nerd?" He asked obnoxiously.

Thomas got red and embarrassed. Still, we ignored him and walked away. When we left the theatre, I wanted to yell at Allison for using Thomas, but I couldn't with Thomas nearby. They walked to their car, and I drove Steph home. I walked her to her house and kissed her in the pouring rain on her porch before

I drove away. I put on Richard Marx's rock version of "Should've Known Better," and was getting flashbacks of working out as a child, my knee injuries, my football games, kissing Steph, and going up and down the hill with the stone. I thought about how I had been the good guy my entire life but was tired of letting the bad guys win. I was tired of bullies and bad boys coming out victorious. I thought about how I should have known better than to get involved with a mean person like Allison Hanson.

Before I went home, I knew I needed to go to Allison's house. It was still raining when I parked in her driveway. I rang her doorbell, and she answered with only a towel covering her body and a towel wrapped around her head. She was blasting Chicago's power ballad "Explain it to My Heart" in her house and looked very happy to see me.

"Drew!" she said as she tried touching me flirtatiously. I was just about to get dressed. Guess what I'm listening to? I love Chicago like you. Please come in. I'm actually all alone," she said as she stroked my shoulder and looked like she wanted to kiss me.

Although I still found Allison extremely attractive on the outside, her self-absorbed personality was way too much of a turn-off for me. I also knew she was only trying to get into Chicago songs to impress me.

"No, we need to talk," I said angrily.

I closed the door behind me, went in, and took a deep breath.

I looked at her and said, "I know you have been using Thomas just to be near me. When will you understand that I don't like you like that anymore? I liked you so much last year, but you broke my heart, and Steph picked up the pieces. I'm with Steph. I love Steph," I told her point blank.

"But...look how hot I am," she said as she was about to remove the towel from her body. But before she could get the towel off, I shut the door in her face and walked out. I could still hear Chicago's powerful breakup song "Explain it to My Heart" coming from her house. The lyrics, "Explain it to my heart, it's better that we're over now, tell me one more time this is the way it's supposed to be, tell me that I'm better off without you, how it's better to forget about you, darling, I understand, now won't you please explain it to my heart," definitely defined my situation with Allison as I could hear her sobbing on the other side of the door. I knew that I was better off without Allison Hanson.

I felt bad that I was mean to her, but I needed to stand up for myself, Steph, and Thomas. It hurt me to break her heart like that, but I knew it had to be done for her to get to the point. I also remembered how badly she broke my heart the school year before. I then blasted Chicago's "If She Would Have Been Faithful..." and drove away. It was the perfect song for the moment because it was about how if the first girl were faithful to the guy, he would have missed out on the second girl. That is exactly how I felt. If Allison never picked Shane over me, I would never have found my beloved Steph. When I got home, I texted Steph that I was home and that I handled Allison. I felt good that I handled Allison, but I knew I had to take care of Hitt the next day, which would be a daunting challenge.

CHAPTER 17: BORN FOR THIS MOMENT

It was time for our first home game of the season at St. Andrews, under the lights against Shane Hitt and the St. Greg's Giants. For me, though, it was more than just a game; it was personal. I was tired of letting Shane Hitt bully people and get away with it. As I ran out of the locker room, I gave my parents and Steph a thumbs-up.

When we were lined up for the National Anthem, Hitt was directly across the field from me. We gave each other an intense glare throughout the entire National Anthem, which reminded me of how Rocky looked at Ivan Drago in *Rocky IV*. When the National Anthem was finished, Hitt pointed to me and screamed, "You're going down!" I gave him a dirty look and shook my head.

We ended up winning the coin toss, and our team chose to receive the ball first. Our marching band was playing Chicago's classic "25 or 6 to 4" to start the game, motivating me even more. "The kickoff was kicked right to me, and I shot off like a bullet once I caught it in the air. I made great juke moves and ran for about 40 yards until my teammate missed a block. Hitt came in and nailed me extremely hard on my left side. When he tackled me to the ground, he gave me an extra push and screamed, "You suck!" The ref heard him and threw the flag for unsportsmanlike conduct. It hurt like crazy, but I was proud of my run.

On the next play, Coach McDuff called a pitch sweep to the left side. I caught the pitch and got a superb block from the slot receiver. I then made a piercing cut on the safety, and I was in the clear. Hitt was playing middle linebacker, and after he shed off a few blockers, he came gunning for me. I could sense him in my vision, and as he came in, he tried to take out my bad knee.

To avoid the hit, I gave him a strong, stiff arm to the head, causing him to fall over. I then had one more man to beat: the free safety. I did another excellent juke move on him and sprinted into the end zone. I could hear the place erupt with excitement.

I had scored many touchdowns in my lifetime but that was one of the most exciting ones that I had scored. Our band started to play the St. Andrew's fight song "Fly Away" as I ran past an embarrassed Shane Hitt, who was still on the ground, ashamed of himself. Although I felt like rubbing it in, it wasn't my style to gloat. I let my playing do all of my talking for me. I believed that if you had to tell someone how good you are, then you really aren't that good.

When I returned to the sidelines, I removed my helmet and saw Steph and my parents clapping. The entire school was so excited. I thanked my lineman for superb blocking, and Coach McDuff said I did great. Then, Allison had to make her way over to congratulate me. I thanked her and was happy she was no longer wearing my number on her cheek. I was also glad that she didn't seem to be mad at me for closing the door in her face.

Suddenly, I heard lots of cheering from the other sideline. I turned around and saw Shane Hitt running for a 50-yard touchdown run. He played both linebacker and running back, and he scored right after I did. I knew he would not give up, so I strapped my helmet back on and returned to the field. I ran the ball six times for 45 yards on the next drive. I then scored a 25-yard touchdown run on a draw play. A draw is when the quarterback drops back like he will throw a long pass and then hands me the ball to fake out the defense. Tashawn Washington got a few carries at fullback but got no yardage. Coach McDuff knew I had the hot hand and kept feeding me the ball.

I had two touchdowns, and we were up 14-7. But again, St. Greg answered back, and Hitt and I kept exchanging touchdowns like a ping-pong match. It ended up being a tie score of 28-28 at halftime. My knee was aching from the excessive running, so I iced it at halftime. Hitt purposely gave me a few knee shots to try and injure me more, but it didn't hurt that much. It was my first ever game in which I scored four touchdowns, and Hitt also scored four, but I knew that my statistics did not matter. The only thing that mattered was beating Shane Hitt and the St. Greg's Giants.

At halftime, my dad came into the locker room to check on my knee and tell me what an awesome job I was doing. He told me to keep running hard. I thanked him and said I still had a whole half left of football. I knew it would be one of my life's toughest games.

The third quarter was a defensive struggle. Despite getting some good yardage, both teams were shut out. It was still 28-28 with less than 1 minute left in the 4th quarter. Unfortunately, St. Greg's had the ball, and they were driving the football down the field. With 25 seconds left, Hitt caught a long pass and marched into the end zone for a Giant's touchdown. Fortunately, they missed the extra point, so they were beating us only 34-28. The bad news was that only 6 seconds left in the game.

I knew that if we lost, we would fall to 0-2 in the year, and I could not lose to Hitt. I needed to return the kickoff for a touchdown to win the game. Coach McDuff knew the Giants would not kick the ball to me, but he instructed whoever got it to pitch it back to me. Our entire stands were chanting, "Dreeeew!" It was such a huge change. The week before, I was "booed", and here I was getting "Drew!"

The Giants kicker kicked it short like we thought he would. The ball went right to our linebacker, who quickly pitched the ball back to me, as Coach McDuff instructed him to do. When I got the ball, a swarm of Giants were about to tackle me. They were coming at me like a flock of birds heading south for the winter. I had no choice but to reverse my field entirely. At that moment, everything just slowed down for me. I felt like I was running for my life. I refused to be tackled and made various moves from jukes, spins, and stiff arms on each Giant player. I did whatever I could to avoid getting tackled, and only one more Giant had a chance to tackle me. Of course, it was Shane Hitt.

Unfortunately, I was not able to cut on him because of where he was, so I had to lower my shoulder, drive my legs, and run him over. I thought about all of the times he was a jerk to me and all of the nasty things that he said. I envisioned that he was the stone, and I was pushing it back up the mountain. I kept driving my legs until I ran over him and sprinted full steam into the end zone. The crowd erupted once more and they were screaming my name in excitement.

We then had to kick the game-winning extra point. Luckily, we had one of the best high school kickers. Our kicker, Steve Buehler, made the game-winning extra point, and our whole team ran onto the field. My team lifted me in the air and carried me off the field. Once I was off, I ran over to Steph and hugged and kissed her.

"I love you so much," Steph whispered to me.

I saw Hitt walking away, and he was so devastated that he kept his helmet on to hide his dejected face. It felt great to get revenge on him, but I did have class, so I went over to him to tell him that he played a great game. He saw me walk toward him, so he ran right off the field in embarrassment. My parents hugged me and told me how proud they were of me. My dad told me he couldn't wait to see it on video.

A reporter then approached me and asked if he could interview me. I told him that he could and when he asked what it felt like to play so well and win the game for my team I told him that my blockers were responsible for my huge game. I thanked them, my coaches, and my fellow teammates. I was then awarded player of the game and player of the week. It was definitely one of the best games of my life.

Unfortunately, my body was not feeling as fabulous as my mind. My body was killing me, especially my legs. It was crazy how I could play so well with a torn ACL. I entered the locker room so my dad could take my brace off. Coach Smith walked by us and asked if I was injured with a furious look on his face. It looked like he wanted me to be hurt. He didn't even tell me that I played a good game.

"No, I'm just taking my brace off," I told him confusedly.

Even with Coach Smith's behavior, nothing was going to keep me down after that game. I pushed my stone back to the top, and I was at an all-time high. Luckily, I could stay up for a short time to come. I knew wonderful things were ahead, and I could not wait for them to take shape.

CHAPTER 18: WE CAN LAST FOREVER

My family celebrated the victory by going to Friendly's for ice cream. I had such a fantastic time with the people that I loved most. I wished that night with my family and girlfriend could have lasted forever. Even after that night ended, my highs did not.

The following week, the team moved Tashawn Washington back to tight end, making me the only starting running back. I also made the cover of the newspaper for my stellar game. The headlines read "Russo Rules," and the article talked about how I scored five touchdowns and led my team to victory over the Giants. I was getting a lot of nice attention in school, which felt excellent.

The football season was going wonderful. We ended up destroying our next three opponents, and I scored a total 200 yards in those games. I did not get a lot of carries because McDuff loved to pass, but I still helped my team win. My knee was holding up, and I was getting closer to achieving my goal of playing an entire season with a torn ACL. I was also doing excellent in school and made the honor roll.

My relationship with Steph was flourishing, and surprisingly, so was Thomas and Allison's friendship. Allison was struggling in school, so she asked Thomas to tutor her. At first, she used him to get near me and to tutor her for free, but later on, she started to see Thomas for who he was as a person. I found that out one night at the movies.

Steph and I went to the movies again with Thomas and Allison. When I got her alone, I confronted her.

"You know, Allison, I'm sick of you using Thomas! He may be a nerd, but he is a lovely guy! When are you going to stop being so shallow and stop liking people for only their looks and their athletic ability?! When are you going to start liking people for their personality and character?!"

She was so stunned that her mouth was wide open, and she did not even respond. It looked like she knew I was right, and when Thomas came out of the bathroom, we all walked out of the theatre together. Thomas held the door for Allison like a gentleman, and I was shocked because Allison finally noticed. When she complimented him that he was a gentleman, Thomas was so flattered that he wasn't even paying attention to where he was walking and almost walked into a car.

They ended up driving home together, and the next week, Thomas claimed that they were getting much closer. According to Thomas, Allison kissed him in her room when he was tutoring her. I didn't believe it until they officially announced they were dating on Facebook. Allison was made fun of so badly and everyone said dating Thomas would cost her the Homecoming Queen, but she did not care. She stood up for Thomas, and I was proud of myself for talking some sense into her.

Thomas and Allison seemed happy and made a lovely couple. Steph and I loved going on double dates with them, and we all became really close friends. It was incredible how Thomas changed so much, as well. He went from being really nervous and shy to calm and kind of even cool. He wasn't nervous around Allison or anyone anymore. It was amazing how self-confidence and a girlfriend could change a man so much. Although it changed Thomas, he still wasn't popular enough to get nominated for Homecoming King. Shockingly enough, I was nominated for the Homecoming court. Even though I was really quiet, I made it because I was so popular in football. Allison also made the court, even though she dated Thomas. Although we became friends, it would have been awkward if we were both nominated for King and Queen.

It was Homecoming week and there were prep rallies and

a lot of hype. I wanted to withdraw from the court because I hated the attention, but nobody wanted me to. It was finally time for the halftime ceremony; unfortunately, Allison and I both won King and Queen. Although Steph said she was okay with it, I could tell that her facial expressions bothered her a little. I hated having to pose for pictures with Allison, and although she said that she moved on with Thomas, I could tell that she still had some feelings for me. Thomas also seemed a little jealous during the pictures.

When it came time for the homecoming dance the next night, I was required to have one dance with Allison. Steph understood, but Thomas looked extremely angry. Allison and I slowly danced to the song "Next Time I Fall" by Peter Cetera and Amy Grant.

She looked into my eyes with the look she had when she liked me. "This is how I always thought it would be, except I always thought we would be dating," she said.

"Allison, you had your chance and blew it. I love Steph, and you've got Thomas now", I said calmly and collectedly.

"I know I'm sorry. You are right; I do love Thomas."

She turned and saw Thomas dancing with Steph, and then she turned back to me.

Before she could say anything, I asked her, "Do you really love Thomas?"

She sighed. "At first I didn't. But now, I am actually falling in love with him. He just doesn't have what you have, she said.

"Well, those things don't always matter. He is smarter than me and has so much heart." "Don't give up on him just because of superficial stuff," I told her.

She smirked. "You know, you are so right," she said.

She leaned in, kissed me on the cheek, and quoted the song "Next time I fall in love, it will be with you."

I smiled, and she asked, "Maybe we can be together in the next life?"

"Maybe," I responded with a smile.

She then went over to Thomas, who had just finished his dance with Steph. We switched dance partners, and Chicago's "We Can Last Forever" began playing. I went up to Steph and kissed her right on the lips.

"What was that for," she asked, a little annoyed because she had to watch me dance with Allison.

"I missed you so much," I told her.

"I missed you too. How was Allison? She asked with a disgusted tone in her voice.

"She's coming along. She is falling in love with Thomas."

She smiled, and we both enjoyed our dance to Chicago's beautiful song. It was incredible looking into Steph's eyes while slow dancing with her and hearing Jason Scheff sing, "Every little look inside your eyes, is all it takes to make me realize, we can last forever, every little moment we can share, gonna let you know how much I care, I'll always be there." I truly felt that Steph and I were going to last forever like the song said.

At the end of the night, we hung out with Thomas and Allison. Despite the awkwardness at first because of the dance, we all had a good time. Things were going so great for the 4 of us, but unfortunately, things would soon take a turn for the worse.

CHAPTER 19: HEART IN PIECES

That Saturday night after the dance, I walked Steph around the block of my house so she could get her car. As I mentioned, my neighborhood was getting very violent at night, so I ensured that Steph made it to her car safely. We held hands and were listening to the beautiful song "Kiss from a Rose" by Seal. The lyrics "You became the light on the dark side of me," really related to me because Steph was always my light. Just as she was getting into her car, I heard a scream. I turned and saw two large males beating up a little guy down the street. It was too far away to make out who the people were. I told Steph to lock her car doors and call the police.

I sprinted as fast as I could to the helpless victim. Steph was screaming at me to come back, but I could not stay there and let that poor man get beat up. At that point, the little man was down on the ground, and they were still attacking him. I ran faster than I had ever run before, but I was too late.

As soon as I got there, the guys took off running. I wanted to chase after them but the guy who had gotten beat up was lying in the street bloodied and bruised. Even in the darkness, I could tell he was in horrible shape. Steph came driving her car down the road to where we were. She told me that the police and ambulance were on their way. My heart sank when I bent down and saw that the man beaten was my dear friend Frankie Rossi. His face had blood all over it and his glasses were cracked.

I could not understand how anyone could beat up Frankie. He was the nicest guy that you could ever meet. I got down and put my aching knees on the rugged street to hold his hand. Steph and I were both trying to comfort him. We told him that we loved him and that he would be okay. Steph started crying and it made me cry too.

Frankie was in so much pain and he tried to talk. "Drew is that you? I'm in. I'm in so much pain. Can you play Chicago for me?"

"Of course Frankie. We love you and you are going to be okay." I told him while getting my iPod out. I played one of his favorite songs "Colour My World" and sang along to it while trying to fight back my tears.

"Now that you're near, promise your love, that I've waited to share, and dreams, of our moments together, colour my world, with hope of loving you." Steph and I sang along and Frankie actually cracked a smile.

The police and ambulance finally showed up after about 2 minutes. They rushed him to the local hospital that was down the road. Steph and I followed the ambulance to the hospital and I called my mom to tell her to contact Frankie's parents to tell them what had happened.

At the hospital, we found out that Frankie was stable, but he had broken his nose, ribs and had severely injured his spine. They told us he could have been killed if it were not for me scaring the men away. The worst news was that there was a chance that he might never be able to walk again.

I was so grateful that he was alive but angry because I could not catch the monsters that did that to him. I told the cops everything that I knew, but I could not make out their faces in the dark. I hoped that when Frankie woke up, he could describe what they looked like. What's more, those monsters only stole $3 from him. They beat him up like that for $3!

I felt helpless, as did Steph. Frankie was her friend just as much as he was mine. I wanted to go find the guys who did it and get revenge for Frankie, but I knew it would be impossible to find out who they were without Frankie's assistance.

Afterward, I went to the hospital Chapel with Steph and talked to God. I was so mad at Him for letting Frankie suffer, but

I still asked him to allow Frankie to walk again. I was baffled, though.

"How could God let such a horrible thing happen to such a nice guy?"

I sat there looking at Jesus on the cross and could not understand why this was all happening.

After we got back from the Chapel, my parents insisted that we all go home and get some rest. I drove Steph home and we kissed each other before she left. We were both emotional and had tears in our eyes. I didn't feel like going home, though, so I drove over to St. Andrew's at around midnight to let out my frustration.

When I was upset, I did what I liked to do: work out. Working out always made me feel better and relieved my stress. I played the songs "There and Back Again" by Daughtry, "Crazy" by Seal, and "Heart in Pieces" by Chicago as I ran about 100 sprints in the sandpit and did about 100 pull-ups altogether. Sweat and tears blended together as I sobbed for Frankie while trying to finish my workout.

After the pull-ups, I went down the hill to attempt to run, but I broke down at the bottom and just sat there sobbing for Frankie while listening to Chicago's orchestral piece, "The Inner Struggles of a Man" and "Mickey" from *Rocky III.* Here I was literally sitting at the bottom of this vast hill sobbing and I realized that I truly was on the bottom of the hill that time.

Before, I thought having a torn ACL was the worst news of my life, but I experienced my first real tragedy, and I did not know what to do. I then remembered my dad's speech about Sisyphus and how everyone gets to the bottom at some point in their lives. I realized that I could either stay there at the bottom and give up or I can get back up and become a better person. I could not do anything to change what happened to Frankie. But I could get back up and try my best to fix it. I then got my cell phone out and took a picture of me sitting at the bottom of the hill so that I could remember how low I got. I made a promise to myself that if I was ever this down again, I would always stand back up. I then stood up and ran 20 sprints up the hill.

I then went to the field and pushed the sled without equipment on. I shoved the sled down the field as I kept picturing Frankie getting beat up. The anger made me push the sled faster than I had ever pushed it. I envisioned that the sled was the Stone of Sisyphus, and I was pushing it back up.

I stayed at the St. Andrew's field for about 2 hours that night. I finally got back in my Jeep Wrangler and put on Chicago's newest song, "Feel," because the lyrics fit my situation. "Your heart is cold, your soul is numb, you don't like who you've become, you've played the game and paid the cost for long enough, so grab the reins, take the wheel, lose what's not and keep what's real, it's not too late, just close your eyes and feel." I felt so lost and finally got back home at around 2:30 am.

When I arrived home, I realized I must have lost my cross necklace while running at St. Andrew's. My parents had given that to me for my Confirmation and I had worn it every day since. I thought it fell off while running and doing pull-ups, but I was too tired to go back to look for it. My knee was also very sore from running to Frankie without my knee brace, so I iced my knee down. I was drenched in blood, sweat, and tears, so I took a hot shower and I cried myself to sleep at around 3:00 am.

I went back to look for the cross necklace in the morning but could not find it anywhere. I felt terrible that I lost it, but I was more concerned about Frankie, who we managed to see awake that day. He looked so hurt, and tears were flowing down his face when he saw Steph and I enter his hospital room. He put his hand out slowly, and I shook it.

In his weak voice, he said, "You guys are my heroes. So, um... what movie are we gonna see next?"

Steph and I both gave him a gentle hug and told him that he could pick the movie soon. We visited Frankie in the hospital every single day and watched his favorite television shows with him. We also played his favorite Chicago songs for him. One of his favorites was the song "Now More Than Ever." The lyrics really made me emotional because they sang, "Now I need you, more than ever, no more crying, we're together." We were so happy to be back together with Frankie after we almost lost him. He was doing a little better, and we enjoyed spending quality time with him.

Steph and I were getting a lot of publicity in the newspaper for saving Frankie. Everywhere we went, people were talking about the heroes we were. Although flattered, I still felt like I should have done more. Honestly, I did not care if I got famous for saving Frankie or if the kids at school started treating me like a hero. I just wanted to catch the criminals to get justice for Frankie.

I did learn something from Frankie's tragedy. I felt sorry for myself when I first tore my ACL, but I finally realized that so many people have it worse than I do. Many people have cancer, diseases, and many other illnesses that are much worse than a torn ACL.

Also, for the first time in my life, I had doubts about my faith. I always believed that God was great, but I was so angry at Him for allowing that to happen to Frankie, who was the sweetest guy in the world. I thought that with all of the symbolic dreams I had been having, losing my cross necklace may have symbolically meant that I was beginning to lose my faith in God. I knew I didn't want to give up on Him and had to overcome the troubling times to find my faith again.

Unfortunately, because of Frankie's attack, I was not ready for our next game against the Harrison Hornets. And neither was my team for the matter. Harrison was undefeated, and they were looking to destroy us. The Hornets hadn't beaten us in 11 years and were our arch-rivals. They were even angrier with us because our team was getting tons of publicity from me saving Frankie's life. After what had happened with Frankie, football did not seem as important as it used to seem, and I just wasn't mentally ready for the game.

Harrison outran us, out-passed us, out-tackled us, out-blocked us and out-coached us. It was one of the worst games I ever played. Although the offensive line didn't block for me well, I also made some horrible mistakes. The biggest mistake was when I fumbled on a pitch sweep. I was running with the ball, and the defender stripped it from behind me to recover the football. Both Coach McDuff and Coach Smith screamed at me when I came off of the field. It was the angriest Coach McDuff had ever gotten with me. They thought that I was playing so poorly that they decided to bench me and put in Tashwan Washington at running back. He had a good game, but our team still ended up getting destroyed 42-14. Washington finished the game with a great 106 yards. At that time, it seemed I would lose my starting running back job.

It was not a very good week for me, and the next week was even worse. Our team won, but I only played one play in the entire game. I was a three-year varsity starter who went from being heroic to a bench player because I had one lousy game. I could not believe that after all I had done for the team, they played me in one lousy play.

We won that game 47-41. Washington had three touchdowns and ran for another 100-yard game. He was the team's new leading man, and many of our fans loved him. Coach Smith was so happy that he was starting over me and rubbed it in my face every chance he could.

I just stood there on the sidelines with my helmet on, feeling so ashamed. It was unbelievable how I could go from being a hero one minute to a nobody the next. I always had to prove myself despite everything I did for my school. I was even more embarrassed looking at my poor parents and girlfriend sitting there in silence. My dad wanted to tell McDuff and Smith off, but I told him to wait because I wanted to earn my spot back.

A part of me thought about quitting and getting the surgery early but I knew that I had to fight back. I had gone too far to give up. I pushed the stone to the top once before and just because it was dropping, I could not let it fall to the ground. I needed to come back with a vengeance and take back what was mine.

CHAPTER 20: SOMETHING'S COMIN', I KNOW

Our next game was against a very tough team called the Thompson Thunder. Thompson was in my home city of Trenton, and the school was located in the violent part of it. My dad taught there, so he knew they had many players with criminal records on their team. As of then, they were undefeated and had a superstar lineman named Terrance Rex. His nickname was T-Rex, and he was one of the top recruits in the Nation. He was about 6'6" and 320 pounds. T-Rex was intimidating, and I knew I had to be up for the challenge. On the bus ride there, I listened to Chicago's Rap Rock song "Sleeping in the Middle of the Bed Again" and "Killer" by Seal to pump me up.

Things were looking up for me because Coach McDuff told me that I would be getting some playing time that week, but Washington would still be the starter. Even though I wouldn't be the starter, I would get to prove myself again. I knew I had to make the most of my opportunity, but Frankie's recovery was the most exciting part of the week. Although his memory was a bit blurry, and he did not remember what the guys who beat him up looked like yet, he was doing a lot better health-wise. They said that he might be able to walk again with enough physical therapy and healing. He was cleared and ready to leave the hospital in a wheelchair. His parents took him to see me play Thompson.

I wanted so much to play my best game for Frankie. I gave him my old practice jersey to wear, and I really wanted to score a touchdown for him. Seeing him show up to the game in the wheelchair got me choked up. I was still so angry at the guys who did that to Frankie, and I wanted to channel my anger and use it to destroy the Thompson defense.

Before the game, T-Rex ran over to our sidelines, took his helmet off, and trash-talked to our fans. His coaches had to grab him and bring him back to their side, but before T-Rex left, Frankie noticed something. As T-Rex was screaming curse words and saying, "I'm gonna kill you," Frankie started putting his hands on his head and was freaking out.

He was screaming, "That's the guy who beat me up!"

He was pointing to T-Rex, but T-Rex did not even realize it. His parents asked him if he was positive that T-Rex was the guy, and he said he was. At first, he could not remember his face, but after seeing T-Rex, he was sure it was him. Frankie also had a flashback to when he got beaten, and T-Rex said, "I'm gonna kill you" to Frankie before I got there.

My dad heard Frankie and ran to the field to tell me about it. I was so furious that I felt like running over to T-Rex and punching him. My dad said that Frankie's dad called the police to get to the game. He told me not to do anything dumb and take it out on T-Rex in the game before the police arrived.

"Here's your biggest chance to get revenge for your friend Frankie. And you can do it legally. Let's do this," he said as he hugged me and wished me luck.

I had never felt so angry in my entire life, and I knew I had to play my absolute best game to get vengeance for Frankie. Before the game, I asked Coach McDuff if I could say something to the team. He nodded yes, so I got up, breathed, and turned to my teammates.

"Hey, guys. I don't say much, but I need to say this. The man who got beat up a few weeks ago, Frankie Rossi, is here today watching, and he just recognized that T-Rex was one of the guys who beat him up so badly that he's in a wheelchair. Please don't say anything until the cops get here, but let's destroy these guys. We have to get revenge for Frankie. Let's do it legally and beat the crap out of him in the game until the cops take him away."

The response I got from the team was terrific. We put our hands in a circle and screamed, "Win for Frankie!"

Just a few moments later, we started playing the game. I played football like a man possessed, returning the opening kickoff for a touchdown. I outran every player on the field, even with my knee brace. I was so angry that I would not let anyone tackle me. Tashawn Washington injured his foot, so I played the rest of the game as the only running back.

Our team was destroying the Thunder. Our line was blocking better than ever, and our right tackle, Jim Jenson, was giving T-Rex a brutal beating on almost every play. On one play, though, T-Rex gave Jenson a good spin move, and he came shooting in to tackle me. I saw T-Rex coming towards me and thought about how Frankie was lying there helpless and bloody because of him. I used every strength to give him a powerful, stiff arm to the head to make him fall into another player.

The game's best moment came on a pass play when my assignment was to block T- Rex. As soon as our quarterback, Andrew Brady, called hike, I charged at him with every force of strength I had. I kept imagining him beating up Frankie, and I was so livid at him. I came so hard and fast that I somehow took him down. I was only 175 pounds, and he outweighed me by almost 200 pounds, but I had so much anger in me that I was able to destroy him. I hit him so hard that he fell down like a ton of bricks.

Our sidelines went wild as Brady hit our receiver on a 60-yard touchdown pass.

After blocking T-Rex, I said, "That was for Frankie."

I could tell that he knew what I was talking about, but he stayed on the ground in pain and in shock. Frankie was excitedly screaming as T-Rex remained in pain for a moment.

When I got off the field, Frankie was chanting my name. Moments later, I saw the cops talking to Mr. Rossi. The game finally ended, and we beat the Thunder 45-0. It was one of our best games ever, and as we were shaking hands with them, we all saw the cops taking T-Rex away in handcuffs. T-Rex gave me the dirtiest look, but I didn't care because he got what he deserved. The police did end up proving that he did beat up Frankie, but they could not catch his accomplice yet, and he refused to tell anyone who it was.

I finished that game with 189 yards and four touchdowns. Frankie hugged me and thanked me as I told him I did that all for him. I then gave him the game ball. Steph and my parents embraced me and told me how proud they were of me. I was so happy that I was able to get revenge on T-Rex. After the game, Coach McDuff told me I would be the starting running back again. I proved that I was the starting running back once and for all; that was how it had to stay.

CHAPTER 21: MORE WILL BE REVEALED

I ended up being in more sports articles after the Thompson game. Many sports reporters interviewed me and made me feel like some type of hero because I got revenge on T-Rex. There was also a really nice picture of me and Frankie in the paper.

I also gained so much respect from my peers at school. I could not even go to a public place without being noticed. Steph and I went on a double date with Thomas and Allison to a movie, and the young kids asked me for my autograph. Thomas, Allison, and Steph laughed at my newfound fame.

After I signed an autograph for a kid, Allison jokingly asked me for my autograph, and we all laughed. It was incredible how much Allison changed after dating Thomas. She proved that she was actually a sweet person. Steph and I both came to like her very much, and she became one of our best friends. My mother always told me that mostly everyone has some form of good in them and that I should try to find or see the good in everyone. Allison did have a lot of good in her. It just took her falling in love with Thomas for us to see it and for her to find it in herself. She no longer liked people for their looks, fame or money, but for their inner beauty.

That night, when I got home from the movies, I got a call from a local sportswriter, who asked me if he could interview me about the upcoming game against the Snyder Spartans. It was going to be a human interest story because ironically, Andrew Brady's dad, Steve, was the quarterback for Snyder in 1977. My dad was the running back, and our offensive coordinator, Peter's dad, was the head coach. The local paper wanted to write an article on how we were going to play our father's former team 30 years later.

Before the writer asked me about the game against Snyder, he asked about my knee. "You always wear that bulky knee brace. What exactly is the injury to your knee?" He asked me, and I paused for a moment to think.

I had been lying to everyone for almost half a year and was sick and tired of it. It was the last game of the regular season, and we were 6-2 with a clinched playoff spot. I couldn't lie anymore.

So I revealed my secret and told him the entire story about how I tore my ACL in the spring and had to keep it a secret to protect myself. I told him what the doctor had told me, that there was a zero percent chance that anybody could play football with a torn ACL. I told him how I had worked so hard in the weight room and how I had been able to prove him wrong thus far. The sportswriter was in shock. He could not believe I was playing so well with a torn ACL. He asked me if I could give him permission to write an article about it. I thought about it and told him that he could. He told me that the article would come out the next day, and then he would interview me and my father again about the Snyder article. He said the ACL one was way more interesting, so he had to write that one first. The writer acted like he hit gold with the torn ACL article.

After I got off the phone with the sportswriter, I walked into my father's room and confessed what I had done. Surprisingly, he wasn't angry at me. He said that it was time to come clean and that I would be getting so much more publicity now.

The next morning, I woke up to get the paper, and I saw my picture on the cover page running the football with my cumbersome knee brace on. The headlines read, Indestructible, St. Andrew's RB Russo confesses to playing the entire season with torn ACL. It was an amazing article about how hard I worked in the weight room and how my dad developed the idea of knee brace Velcro. It talked about how the doctor said there was a 0 percent chance a running back could play a whole year with torn ACL and how I proved him wrong. But most importantly, it talked about the Stone of Sisyphus reference and how I kept falling down and coming back up.

I have had many articles written about me in the past, but that one was definitely the best and the one that I was most proud of. Everyone in school was talking about the article and congratulating me. They were saying how tough I was, and I was very flattered. Coach McDuff also called me into his office, as I was expecting he would. I just really hoped that he wouldn't be mad at me for lying to him. I nervously walked into his office.

He told me to sit down and then pulled out the article, "You know you are one tough S.O.B.," he said with a huge smile on his face.

"I'm not happy that you lied to me, but I understand why you did it. I am so proud of you for playing with this injury. You are truly a warrior son," he said as he got all choked up and shook my hand.

"Now get back to class Rambo, I mean Russo." It was an ode to one of my favorite Stallone characters, the ultimate tough guy named Rambo.

It was amazing how my nerves turned to excitement so quickly. Unfortunately, I bumped into Coach Smith leaving McDuff's office. He gave me one of his evil stares, but before I knew it, he shook my hand.

"Way to be a tough guy." He actually cracked a smile as he said that. I was surprised that he was finally respecting me. I thought that if there was good in Allison then maybe there was good in Coach Smith too.

When I got to History class, the Vice Principal got on the intercom and announced that ESPN was on the phone looking for me and wanted to interview me. My class was cheering and treating me like some superstar. I went down to talk with ESPN and found out that they wanted to interview me about playing all season with a torn ACL. Things could not have gotten any better.

The next night, my parents drove me and Steph to New York for my first ESPN interview. I was so nervous because the entire world would hear my story. To try and calm me down, I listened to Chicago's song "Our New York Time," which was about New York. I hoped that I would give them a good and interesting interview. Luckily, I took a public speaking class in my freshman year of high school, which I hoped would help.

It was like a dream come true when we got to the studio. I was going to be on ESPN, where all of my favorite sports heroes sat to give their interviews. They interviewed my mom, my dad, Steph, and finally, me. I was really proud of the interview that I gave them, and I could not wait to see it on television.

It came on ESPN two days later, and of course, we recorded it on an old-school videotape. I was ecstatic, and it was another moment that I would never forget. When I went back to school, the kids were saying what a fantastic interview it was. Coach McDuff called me into his office and congratulated me on the interview. He said he was so proud to be my Coach and that it was one of the most inspirational ESPN segments he had ever seen. He then said that the sportswriter wanted to do that Snyder interview on me and my dad next. Our last game of the year was Snyder, and they still needed us to do one more interview about that game. At the time that Coach McDuff said that, I had no idea that the upcoming article would end up causing so much controversy.

CHAPTER 22: YOU'RE THE INSPIRATION

That night, when they were interviewing my father about Snyder, the sportswriter asked him, "What was it like playing for Snyder in the 70s?"

"We were just a bunch of hard working kids who loved the game of football so much," my dad said.

When Snyder read the article, they apparently misunderstood what my father was saying. They thought my father was saying that Snyder was not tough currently and that they were tougher back then. This made the current Snyder Spartans furious with our team, especially my father and me.

When it came time for my father and me to take our pictures for the article, we had no idea that Snyder would eventually use the pictures as motivation for the upcoming game. A friend of mine at Snyder told me that they hung pictures of our faces on their locker room wall and drew bad things on them. They used our heads to inspire them to beat us. We actually found it funny, but when it came time for our game, Snyder came to our school extremely angry with us.

Before the game, when Snyder's bus pulled in, my dad was putting my knee brace on by the car. The first guy to come off the bus was their offensive coordinator, Dan Dorney.

When he saw my dad and me, he started screaming, "I guess we aren't as tough as we were in the 70s!"

My dad knew he was referring to the article, and we knew Snyder was fired up. Fortunately for us, their performance did not show their anger. They were pathetic, and I ran all over them. Even though my dad did not say they were better in the 70s, their performance proved that they were much better in the 70s.

We ran into the field blasting Boston's classic rocker "Don't Look Back" and were ready to destroy them.

Then their middle linebacker P.J. Stanton was talking a lot of trash. "First, I'm gonna take you out, and then I'm gonna take your old man out on the sidelines."

Stanton's dad was my dad's rival at Snyder when they were younger, and Stanton was also my rival. He wrestled and played football with me since I was little, and I always beat him. He was a jealous jerk, but when he threatened my father, I was outraged.

On the next play, when I got the ball, I got back at him. I lowered my shoulder and ran him to the ground—the same form of revenge I used on Shane Hitt and T-Rex. My last man to beat on the play was the safety, and I did an incredible juke move on him before I sprinted right into the end zone. Our marching band started to play Chicago's rocking song "Getaway" as we were killing them 28-0.

In the 3rd quarter, I got a pitch sweep, and Stanton took a great angle to attempt to take out my legs. It came out that my ACL was torn, so Stanton wanted to injure me even more. He hit my knee fiercely and knocked me right out of bounds. After he hit me, he went after my dad, who was standing on the sidelines by Coach McDuff. He pushed my dad, and as his knee buckled, he fell to the ground in agony. I saw this and was so outraged that I got off the ground as fast as possible and tackled Stanton with all my might after the play.

Stanton got up and tried coming for me. My teammates, Coaches, and refs quickly restrained us, and we were ejected from the game because of our fight. I never condoned this type of violent behavior or getting ejected from a game, but when it came to protecting my family, I would do anything. I was always about following the rules 100 percent, but I learned that sometimes you have to break the rules to protect people if the evil ones do not follow the rules. That was when I thought it was okay for me to break the rules. I wasn't going to let Stanton hurt my father and get away with it.

Coach McDuff understood why I had to do what I did. "I usually don't go for that. But man, seeing you take out Stanton made me feel great. I would have done the same if he had done that to my father. Go in and take care of your dad. The game is won here," Coach McDuff said with a huge grin on his face.

Our athletic trainer and security guard drove us into the locker room on the golf cart, and the crowd cheered for us. "Russos, Russos, ..." they were chanting as the marching band played Chicago's song "To Be Free." I hugged my dad, who thanked me for standing up for him. I could tell that he was in a lot of pain. He already had six knee surgeries from playing football and lifting weights when he was younger. I hoped he didn't require any more surgeries.

My knee was also sore, so the trainer gave us both ice, and we sat there in the locker room with our legs elevated. We were both pleasantly surprised when our beautiful ladies came to visit us. My mom and Steph went into the locker room and hugged us.

They felt sorry for us and sat there, holding our hands in the sweaty and smelly locker room. The fact that they were willing to sit in the disgusting locker room with us really showed their love. They were both big "skeeves," as the Italians would say.

Steph laughed and said, "This romantic moment needs some music."

So she put on Chicago's most famous love song, "You're the Inspiration," and we all started bobbing our heads to the music. I never would have thought that I would be listening to "You're the Inspiration" in our locker room with my dad and both of us would have injured knees, holding our ladies' hands. We were a little embarrassed when our entire team walked in on our little romantic moment and started singing the chorus at the top of their lungs. "You're the meaning in my life; You're the Inspiration."

Steph and my mom quickly told us that they loved us and ran out of there faster than I'd ever seen them run to avoid the team undressing in front of them. The team had great news: They ended up winning the game, and we finished the regular season with a 7-2 record. The bad news was that Coach McDuff told me that league rules indicated that if a player gets ejected from a game, they must sit out the first half of the next game. That meant I would be forced to sit out the first half of the next week. The worst part was that it was our first playoff game against the St. Francis Falcons.

I couldn't believe I had to sit out for the first half, but I knew it was worth defending my father's honor. Unfortunately, my father's knee wasn't doing well. Stanton severely hurt his knee when he gave him that cheap shot, and my father would probably need another surgery.

CHAPTER 23: REMEMBER THE FEELING

The Thursday night before our first playoff game, my dad took my family, Steph, and me to dinner at Amici Milano in Chambersburg. At dinner, my dad announced that he would be getting knee surgery on December 18th, which was the same day that I would be getting my surgery. He chose that day because that was the only available day. We told him that we would be there for him and that we would get through the surgeries together. So, at dinner, we celebrated our family's love and how lucky we were to have each other. My family and girlfriend were truly my life's most important things.

Unfortunately, the next night did not start very well for us. I had to sit out the first half and watch my team get destroyed at our home school. Tashawn Washington started the game for me and was shut out. The whole team was shut out. We could not run, block, pass, or tackle.

We were losing 21-0 at half-time. I knew that my team needed me to play better than I had ever played before if we had any chance at coming back to win the game.

Coach McDuff came over to me with that serious look in his eyes and said, "We need your heart."

So, I used every ounce of my heart to play my very best game. I thought about how T-Rex and his buddy beat Frankie to a pulp and how Stanton hurt my dad. Thinking about them fueled my fire and made me furious. I refused to go down and let anyone stop me. I took my first run of the game, 47 yards for a touchdown. Our crowd went wild, and I finally woke them up and put some scare into the Falcons.

Our defense made a nice stop and we drove it right back down to the red zone on our next possession. I had seven carries for 53 yards on that drive. We scored a touchdown when the quarterback faked the handoff to me, scrambled to the right side, and passed to the tight end, who was wide open in the end zone.

It was 21-14 at the end of the third quarter, but we got scared because St. Francis drove their way back down the field. Luckily, our safety, Jeff Michaels, was able to intercept their pass to give us the ball again. We drove the ball right back down and ended up scoring on a 20-yard pass to tie the game up.

It was tied up with less than a minute left in the game, and it looked like the Falcons would score a touchdown. Their quarterback passed the ball to their receiver, who was wide open in the middle of the field. He caught the ball, and it looked like he was going to score, but then our cornerback chased him down and stripped the ball from him. We then recovered the ball and had 43 seconds left to score a field goal or touchdown.

On first down, our quarterback threw an incomplete pass, but the clock stopped. On second down, our receiver dropped a pass that was right in his hands. It was then third down with the clock stopped at 39 seconds. On 3rd down, our quarterback got sacked in the backfield for a loss of 8 yards. It was then 4th and 18 and the clock was still ticking with under 25 seconds left in the game.

We had to rush to the line, and the quarterback called hike with about 20 seconds left. He was scrambling for his life because the defensive end penetrated the backfield unblocked. I saw that the quarterback was in trouble, so I got open for a short pass. I caught the ball and saw that their cornerback was coming right towards me. I made one of the sharpest cuts that I ever made on him, and he fell right to the ground.

I then saw the outside linebacker coming in from an angle of pursuit. I made a great spin move on him but was still hit on my backside by the middle linebacker. Although I was hit hard, I refused to go down, and I kept driving my legs until he fell off of me. All of those hill runs that I did with the sled on my back paid off, and I drove as if I were running the hills. I then made two more jukes and a stiff arm on my way to the end zone for the touchdown.

Our marching band started to play "Gonna Fly Now" from *Rocky*, and the crowd went insane because we won our first playoff game in 13 years. Coach McDuff hugged me, and then my family, Steph, Thomas, and Allison, came over to congratulate me. I gave Steph a big kiss and told her how much I loved her. She told me she was so proud to be my girlfriend and that I overcame so much to get where I was. It was just an incredible night, and we ended it by celebrating. My parents treated my brothers, Thomas, Allison, Steph, and me to dinner. It was a brilliant way to end a remarkable night.

CHAPTER 24: CRAZY HAPPY

The next day, Thomas, Allison, Steph, and I did community service at a place where people with paraplegia participated in sports events. I had done community service before, but I had not done anything with people with paraplegia.

I got so depressed over tearing my ACL because I wasn't able to walk for a month or two, and these people could never walk again. Some of them were even born like that. I could not imagine never being able to walk, and it made me grateful for what I had.

It was so amazing watching them play sports in a wheelchair, and they participated in many extraordinary events. They were also really competitive.

I thought, "If only some of the guys on my team could have this type of heart and intensity."

I saw that Thomas, Allison, and Steph were just as blown away as I was. We volunteered for about five hours because it was so much fun. We helped them get ready for each sport and made many friends. The most inspirational moment came when an African American boy with paraplegia, around 13 or 14 years old, rolled his way over to me.

He excitedly said, "You're... you're Drew Russo! I'm one of your biggest fans. You're my hero! You're such an amazing football player..."

Tears welled up in my eyes. "Thanks, buddy, but I'm not a hero. You are. You're way tougher than I could ever be."

"Thank you so much," he said.

"What is your name, buddy?" I asked him.

"Lido Jones," he replied.

My eyes lit up when he said Lido. "Were you named after the old song, "Lido Shuffle" by Boz Scaggs, by any chance?" I asked him.

He nodded and said," It's my dad's favorite song."

I excitedly told him that I was a huge Boz Scaggs fan. I thought that maybe it was fate, that I was meant to meet Lido.

Then, I had a great idea: "How would you and your parents like to watch our playoff game this week from our sidelines?"

His happy face turned into sheer awe. "Would you really do that for me?" He asked.

"For you, anything," I told him."

Although I hadn't asked Coach McDuff yet, I knew he wouldn't mind. Lido then asked for my autograph, and I signed a piece of paper at that moment, but I told him I would sign a picture of myself for him before our next game. He got excited, but in my mind, I thought that he was the one who should be signing my autograph.

He was the true hero, and I was sick of our society's worship of the wrong people. I signed the paper, "To a true hero, Lido." As I signed it, I started to sing the old Boz Scaggs song, "Lido, woah woah woah, he's for the money, he's for the show, Lido's a-waiting for the go." Steph, Thomas, and Allison also started singing with me, and Lido smiled so big. We were all really inspired by Lido's big heart.

At the end of the event, I talked to Lido's dad. I told him about the game and that I would drop off the sideline passes at his house before the game. He thanked me, and we talked about our favorite Boz Scaggs songs. They had to leave, but Steph and I hugged Lido goodbye.

Moments later, I had an idea. I went to the head of the event and asked him if he would be interested in having me train the people with paraplegia with weights. He said it was a great idea, but their budget needed to be higher, and they would only be able to afford to pay me a little.

But I quickly replied, "I'm not going to take money for this. I'm not even going to take community service hours for this. I want to do this because I love these guys."

He paused, trying to process my words. Soon, he shook my hand and thanked me. He told me he would work on a schedule and get back to me.

After the event, we decided that, since it was the night before Halloween, the 4 of us would go on a haunted hayride. Fall was my favorite time of year, and I loved the hayrides. Allison, Steph, and I did not get scared much at all. Thomas, on the other hand, was a different story. He was holding on to Allison's arm like he was holding on for his life. He screamed at every goofy goblin, ghost, and witch in costume. The worst of his fears came when a guy with a chainsaw came from behind him. Thomas was so scared that he climbed out of the ride and returned to the car.

Allison was so embarrassed that she chased after him. Steph and I couldn't believe it, but we stayed on and finished the hayride. It was not scary for us, but maybe because we kissed each other for most of it. When we returned to our cars, we saw Allison and Thomas kissing. I could not believe she didn't break up with him after that embarrassing display. It proved that Allison truly loved Thomas.

After the hayride, we were supposed to go to the old Kuser Mansion in our town for a ghost hunt. Steph and I suggested we skip it because it might be too scary for Thomas. Still, the couple insisted they go and that Thomas would be alright. On the way there, we listened to *Casper*, *Hocus Pocus*, and *Addams Family* soundtracks, some of my favorite Halloween movies. When we got to the Mansion, everything was going well at first. Thomas was very quiet but still held on to Allison for dear life.

The ghost hunters explained how to use the equipment. Steph and I had our piece, and Allison and Thomas had theirs. Thomas was wedged between Allison and me, looking as pale as a ghost. The detector could pick up noises. The hunter ironically said that the ghost was saying, "Thomas."

Thomas got so scared that he ran as fast as he could down the stairs and out the door. Of course, Allison ran out after him like the good girlfriend she was. Steph and I finished the tour and had a great time.

When Steph and I walked out on the pitch-dark night, we saw Thomas and Allison kissing again. I could not believe that she still made out with him after another embarrassing display, but I was happy with the person that Allison turned out to be. I did have to mess with Thomas, though. I snuck up on the car, pressed my face to the window, and screamed to scare Thomas. He turned to the window and screamed, too. We all laughed and finished our night by going through my library's secret passageway and watching Hocus Pocus in my attic bedroom tower. My tower ironically looked like the one that Max had in *Hocus Pocus*. It was a memorable night, but I knew it was time to focus on our next game after the Halloween festivities.

Our next game was our last playoff game. We would get to our first State Championship game in 25 years if we won. I was very inspired by visiting the people with paraplegia and I knew that Lido, Frankie, my family, Thomas, Allison, Steph and the entire county would be watching us.

CHAPTER 25: NOTHING'S GONNA STOP US NOW

It was time for our second round of the playoffs against the 5th ranked team in the state, the St. Anne's Angels. St. Anne's destroyed us in the playoffs the year before, and we wanted revenge. Still, they had a lot more talent and were better ranked than us. We weren't even ranked in the top 50 in the state, and we knew that we would have to play our absolute best game in order to beat them.

Coach McDuff let me give sideline tickets to both Lido and Frankie. They were such tough guys, and the fact that they were able to overcome so much in their lives inspired me to want to win the game for them. The game was finally underway, and our team had so much will and confidence that we could hold our own with the Angels.

Unfortunately, the team studied my film and shut me out for most of the game. It did leave our passing game wide open, though. It was a seesaw game because St. Anne's would score a touchdown, and then we would score one right back. I was embarrassed because I literally could not get any yardage. I had five carries for about 11 yards, and I wanted to put on a show for Lido and Frankie, who were both on the sidelines watching me.

At the end of the fourth quarter, it was tied 21-21. We had just turned the ball over on downs because they gave me the ball on 4th and 4, and I came up a yard short. St. Anne's took the ball, and there were less than four minutes left.

Lido saw me walking off the field dejected, so he rolled his wheelchair over to me and said, "Hey, keep your head up. This game's not over yet. Don't be depressed. You can do this, Drew. Win this game for all the people who can't do the things that you can do. The people who don't have the amazing athletic ability you have, the people who can't walk, the people who can't even stand. Being a running back is just like life. In most plays, you get knocked down to the ground hard, but you can't lie down. Just like some days you get knocked down. You must get back up, move on, and prepare for the next play. You can't stay on the ground and sulk. Drew, you always have to be ready to stand. Stand your ground and never back down."

It was amazing how someone that young could say something so motivating, but it was one of the most critical moments of my life. Here I was, sulking about playing a lousy game, and this boy was on the sidelines wishing he could play football. He was just wishing he could walk and even stand. I knew that I had to stop being upset and move on to the next play.

Unfortunately, St. Anne's still had the ball and was driving with only 3 minutes left. I just had to pray that they would turn the ball over on downs, and they eventually did. Our punt returner had just injured his ankle, so Coach McDuff called me to return the punt. Punts were the most nerve-racking thing in football because the returners were the only guys back there, and it was tough to predict where the ball was going, catch it, and avoid the oncoming train of defenders.

My body shook with nerves, but I knew I had to take it to the end zone. I knew at that moment nothing was going to stop me. I was standing back there to return the punt, and I looked over at Lido and Frankie in their wheelchairs. I kept repeating what Lido said, "It's time to stand your ground and never back down." I was more ready than ever. Then, our marching band started to play Chicago's classic song "Make Me Smile," which pumped me up even more.

The Angels punted and the ball was coming right to me but I could see an Angel defender coming very close. Usually when they got that close, you were supposed to fair catch it. A fair catch is when you wave your hand, and the defenders must let you catch it. Once you catch it, you must stop running and the play is dead. Although I should have fair caught it, I knew that I could return the punt, so I was stubborn and caught the punt with the angel defender right in my face. I was able to be quick and did an amazing spin move that avoided him. I then made a cut move to the middle and kept cutting back and forth. It was one of my career's best runs, and I was cutting so much that nobody could tackle me.

I ended up returning the punt 62 yards for a touchdown, and the stadium went crazy. I quickly ran to the sidelines with the ball, gave it to Lido and hugged him.

"Way to stand tall, Drew," he said.

We made the extra point to go up 28-21. There were still 2 minutes left, though, and St. Anne's was getting the ball back. Coach McDuff called me over and told me that our cornerback was injured and that they needed me to play cornerback. I was so nervous because I hadn't played cornerback in about two years. Coach Smith did not want me to play it because he did not trust me, but Coach McDuff overruled him and told me that they needed my speed to cover.

Unfortunately, my first few plays did not go too well. The Angel receiver gave me a juke move and caught an out pass on me. Fortunately, I was able to push him out of bounds. St. Anne's kept driving on us, and although I made few tackles, they kept moving the ball closer to the end zone.

A minute was left, and St. Anne's lined up for the play. I was guarding their fast receiver and he juked me out so bad that my knee buckled and he blew right past me. He caught a 30-yard pass and was heading toward the end zone. I ran as fast as I could, but it was too late. He had scored, and St. Anne's was only down 28-27. I couldn't believe that I let my man score, and I heard Coach Smith yelling at McDuff, "I told you he's not a cornerback."

I knew that the game might have to go into overtime

because of me and St. Anne's lined up to kick the extra point to tie it up. I was still playing cornerback on the right side. For some reason, I had a gut feeling that St. Anne's was going to try and pull something sneaky, and I was right. They faked the kick, their holder rolled to my side of the field and threw a pass to their tight end.

I was able to run as fast as I could to intercept the pass to stop them and seal the game. I then ran as fast as I could to the sidelines and gave the ball to Frankie. He hugged me also, and it was so great to see Lido and Frankie on the sidelines with the balls. They had even become buddies.

My dad and Steph came down and congratulated me. All we had left to do was to take a knee and we were going to the Championship. We went out in victory formation and Brady called hike, took a knee and the clock ran out. We beat the St. Anne's Angels 28-27 and were heading to the State Championship! I couldn't believe it. I had dreamt about going to the State Championship my entire life. I kissed Steph on the lips and gave my parents a big hug. The song from the *Rocky IV* Soundtrack, "The Sweetest Victory," was playing in my head.

The players dumped the water coolers on Coach McDuff's head, and he was soaking wet. Although I only finished with 18 rushing yards, I scored the winning touchdown and ended the game with an interception. I thanked Lido and Frankie for motivating me so much and gave them credit for inspiring me when reporters interviewed me.

After we got cleaned up, my father took my family, Steph, Thomas, Allison, Lido, and Frankie out to eat like always. We really just enjoyed our friendships and celebrated making the Championship. It was truly a night always to remember.

The next day I went back to the center for people with paraplegia and I started my first workout session with them. Steph came with me to help them, and Frankie joined us as well. Frankie was still unable to walk and the doctors were still unsure if he would ever walk again but he worked hard to strengthen his upper body and leg muscles.

My dad had been training me since I was six years old, and I always wanted to be able to train people when I got older. It felt so good to finally be able to help others like my dad helped me. The people with paraplegia had played a lot of sports, but they never lifted weights before. I did a lot of research and checked with my father to ensure that all the exercises were safe for them.

Before we started the workout, we played an icebreaker game. I asked them about their hobbies, favorite foods, movies, music, and sports. Once I got to know them a little bit better, I started introducing every exercise, as well as which body part they worked. I made every person try out each exercise to make sure that they were performing it correctly. They were loving it. Once I felt like they were comfortable with each exercise, I turned on the *Rocky* soundtrack, and we worked our butts off for an hour. They had so much passion, drive, and determination to get in better shape.

The next day at practice, a couple of players were complaining that they were sore and didn't feel like practicing. They wanted to stay in and watch films.

Coach McDuff threw a fit and screamed at them. "This is the championship week and you are complaining!"

So, to prove a point, that night, Coach McDuff took the entire team to work out with the people with paraplegia. Their reactions were priceless, especially when they saw how hard the people worked.

After the intense workout, Coach McDuff talked to them. "So now, if you ever complain about being sore, just think about these people and how hard they work. You guys don't realize it, but you have it made. You are all fantastic athletes on a high school football team in the State Championship. You have a top-notch education and families willing to pay a lot of money for you to attend this school. You have a roof over your head, food, and clothes and you are not sick. You guys are so blessed, so you have no right to complain. This is our championship week, and I want you to give it all you have. Especially you Seniors. You will never get this moment back again, so don't ruin it."

From that moment on, the team was ready for the Championship.

CHAPTER 26: YOU'VE GOT TO BELIEVE

A few nights before our State Championship game, Frankie, Lido, and I did one of our best workouts ever. We were all so pumped about the game, and our excitement showed in our workout. Lido and Frankie wanted to race me in a 100-yard sprint in their wheelchairs as I ran. I gave them a 60-yard head start, of course.

At first, I thought about letting them win, but Lido said, "And don't even think about letting us win."

They wanted to be treated like everyone else, so I gave it everything I had. I strapped my brace up and looked in front of me as Lido and Frankie wheeled over to the starting line. I returned to my track stance and waited for my dad to call out the cadence. He called it, and I exploded off the line. I tried my best to catch them, but I couldn't. They both beat me in the race.

Afterward, I thanked them for pushing me and for being such great friends. They told me how excited they were for the State Championship, and I told them I was too. I worked harder than anyone could, and I knew I just had to give it everything I had.

A few days later, it was game day. I had so many thoughts as I sat on the bus, taking us to our first State Championship game since the 1980s. I put on "No Easy Way Out" from the *Rocky IV* soundtrack and thought about the long road I had traveled to get to where I was. I thought about how I dreamt of winning the State Championship since I was a little kid. I thought about the day I found out that my ACL was torn. I thought about overcoming 3 falls. I thought about Allison shattering my heart, falling in love with Steph, watching Frankie get beat up by T-Rex, and PJ. Stanton injuring my dad.

I had to overcome so much, but the time had come to

accomplish my final major goal of the year. If I could win the State Championship, it would prove that I conquered everything and rolled my stone back up to the top after it had fallen several times. I was a nervous wreck, so I took several tums to calm me down.

I figured that everyone would be just as nervous, but when I looked to my side, I saw our quarterback, Andrew Brady, who did not seem nervous at all. He slept on our bus ride. His sleeping head was leaning on my shoulder and he was even drooling on me. It was gross and awkward, but I didn't know what to do. I couldn't believe that our starting quarterback was so calm that he could actually sleep before the biggest game of our lives.

I guess everyone had their own ways of preparing for a game. I would get so many butterflies in my stomach until I got tackled for the first time. For some reason, once I got tackled in the game, the butterflies would go away and I would be in a groove. I know it's weird to say that pain makes most football players less nervous, but it's true for me and many guys. The entire game of football is painful. It hurts to get hit for an hour and a half. It hurts to bleed and to run so hard on every play. Every body part aches on us, but that is what makes the game so much fun. Football players love to fight through the pain and overcome it to win the game. Games would not be any fun without a challenge.

Luckily, I conquered the pain all season. It was time to put everything on the line for the Championship. We finally got to the stadium, and it was time to enter the locker room. When I left the bus, I heard my family—Steph, Thomas, Allison, Lido, and Frankie—chanting my name. I turned around and waved to them. I really wanted to make them more proud of me.

We all sat in our locker room and waited for Coach McDuff and Coach Smith to come. Unfortunately, when Coach Smith came, he started screaming at us and telling us how this was the most important thing in our lives and how it is do or die. It was pointless, but Coach McDuff came right after him.

"Coach Smith, I highly disagree. This is not the most important thing in your life. Your family, school, your health, community service, and your girlfriends are way more important than this game because that is exactly what it is. It's a game. I know this is the most important game of your life, but you have to settle down guys. I wanna win more than anyone but all we can do is what we have been doing all season and that is to give it our absolute best. We have to put all our blood, sweat, and tears into this game, and if you try your best, I will be so proud of you. Just keep doing what we have been doing all season, and don't overthink this."

Coach Smith then walked into the other room, punched a football dummy, and screamed, "Idiot!" during the speech.

The team laughed, and Coach McDuff rolled his eyes. Coach McDuff knew we were playing the number 1 team in the state and the number 3 team in the nation. They were called the Incarnation Ironmen, and they truly looked like Ironmen. They had 5 Division I recruits. I had been studying their film since we made the playoffs, and I knew that our team would have to roll on all cylinders for us to win the game. One player could not beat that team. Our team would all have to play well if we even had a chance to defeat them.

I got dressed in my football gear, put my lucky armbands on my biceps, and then my dad came in to put on my knee brace.

He hugged me and said, "I know you can do this Drew. You are the toughest, strongest, and best person that I know. Your mother, brothers, Steph, and I are here for you no matter what. Just believe in yourself. Have faith in yourself. Like the Chicago song says, "You've Got To Believe."

My dad's message sunk it. I always thought I had faith and confidence in myself, but honestly, at the start of the year,

I did not at all. I was always getting depressed and doubted if I could accomplish something. That was why I kept getting those nightmares of me falling down the hill with the stone. I kept thinking in my mind that I was falling but that last month, I kept getting reoccurring dreams of me pushing the stone back up to the top. I finally had confidence and faith in myself. It was time to use that to help beat Incarnation and show them I was the true Ironman.

Our team lined up at the entrance of the field and we were anxiously anticipating the PA announcer to call our names before the game. I was looking out at the stadium, and it was crazy how massive it was. It was a professional football stadium, and there were so many people. I couldn't believe that it was all happening. I had dreamt about playing a championship game in a pro stadium since I was young, and I knew I had to make the best of this once-in-a-lifetime opportunity.

They first announced our quarterback, Andrew Brady, and I was announced second.

"At running back, number 22, Drew Russo!" As the announcer excitedly said my name, I got a surge of excitement. For the first time in my life, I actually believed in myself, and ironically, Chicago's pop song "You've Got to Believe" was blasting through the stadium speakers. I knew that it was a sign. There were no doubts. I was Drew Russo, and I was indeed a winner. In most games, I hoped we could win, but in this game I knew that we would win. We were going to win. Although I said that I would prove the doctor wrong and play the whole season with a torn ACL, I had so many doubts in the back of my mind. This time, I had no doubts. I was going to help my team win the Championship, and nobody would stop me. I would not let anyone stop me.

We won the coin toss, and Coach McDuff gave us a pre-game speech. "This is the moment we were all waiting for. Believe in yourselves, and you will win. We are going to win."

Ironically, it was basically the same speech that my dad gave me. We then prayed our usual prayer, Our Lady of Victory, and I went out for the kickoff return. I hoped they would kick it to me, but unfortunately, they fooled us and did an unexpected onside kick. They got the ball back, and Coach Smith screamed at McDuff for not expecting it. We got off to the worst start.

Incarnation scored a touchdown on their first 3 drives. Our defense just could not stop them and our offense could not run or pass. I only got two carries in the first half for a terrible 5 yards. Our passing game was horrible and Brady kept throwing incomplete passes and interceptions. Our team was turning on each other and Coach McDuff and Coach Smith were also turning on each other.

Although there was always bad blood between Smith and McDuff, they started getting along up to that point. We were finally playing team ball, but this game made us go back to what we used to do. We went back to blaming each other, yelling, and arguing, which killed our team. Our defense was blaming our offense for their mistakes, our offense was blaming the defense for their mistakes and the coaches were blaming each other for their mistakes. Before we knew it, we were down 28-3 at halftime.

Although we were down by 21, I knew that we were still going to come back and win the game. I don't know how I knew it, but I had a gut feeling that we were going to win. I just needed to do something that I had wanted to do for a long time. I needed to stop being so shy and talk some sense into my team like I did to Allison Hanson those few months before. Coach McDuff was criticizing our playing and I stood up and raised my hand.

"What is it, Drew?" he asked.

I took a deep breath. "Okay, so I know I never speak up, and I'm really shy, but I need to say something that I should have said two years ago. I'm absolutely tired of you guys turning on each other. We are a team. I know some of us don't like each other, but we are a team and need to learn how to respect and work together. Coaches, it starts with you. I know you guys aren't crazy about each other, but you're teammates as well. You must learn to get along if you expect to win this Championship. If you guys don't listen to each other and get along, then we will lose this football game. This is a team game and it's all of our fault we're getting killed. It's not the offense's fault, the defense's, or the coach's fault. If somebody fumbles or misses a tackle, don't scream in their face. Just tell them to keep their head up and do better the next play. I know that when we were winning, things were going great and we were all getting along. But now, we're getting killed, and we need to work together to win this game. We need to have faith in each other and faith in ourselves. So many people dream about playing football and playing in a pro stadium in a State Championship, but if we don't work together, we will let our biggest chance ever go down the tubes. We need to get off the bench, take each other's hands, and be ready to stand."

The players and Coaches were dead silent. I had no idea what the coaches might do to me after I called them out.

Finally, Coach McDuff said something. "...I'm...sorry. Drew is absolutely right. Let's shake hands and work together. Coach Smith, I'm sorry," McDuff said, putting his hand out for Smith to hopefully shake. At first, Smith hesitated.

Finally, he nodded. "I'm sorry too, Coach," he said as he shook his hand. The entire team was apologizing and shaking each other's hands.

I then screamed, "We are going to win this game! I know we are!" We ran back out on the field with so much fire and passion. We were ready to come back and win the game. Coach McDuff had a clever idea to do the same thing they did to us at the beginning of the game, so we started with an unexpected onside kick and recovered the football.

When we were on offense, Brady faked the handoff to

me and hit our receiver Jennings on a 42-yard touchdown pass. We were only down by 18 points. Although the Ironmen were driving pretty far on their next drive, our cornerback was able to intercept the pass. We had the ball back, and Coach McDuff finally started giving me the ball more. I caught the pitch sweep and could tell that one of the Ironmen was trying to hurt my knee, so I leaped over him. I'm not sure how I did it, especially with a torn ACL and an enormous knee brace on, but I did. I ran for 40 yards, and then, on the next play, Andrew Brady faked the handoff to me and rolled out to the left. Unfortunately, the Ironman defensive end came from behind, stripped the ball from Brady, and recovered it.

We were able to stop the Ironmen on defense and got the ball back. I was able to run the ball 6 times for 50 yards on the next drive. Andrew Brady was able to score a touchdown on a quarterback sneak up the middle and we were only down by 11 points going into the 4th quarter. Our team was congratulating each other and encouraging one other. We then we able to stop the Ironmen offense on the next few drives from scoring.

We were driving down the field with less than 4 minutes left in the game, but we needed to score. It was 3rd and 13, and they were expecting a pass. Coach McDuff decided to do the unexpected and give me a draw handoff. Although there was not much of a hole, I got 11 yards but was 2 yards short of a first down. The linebacker hit my knee hard, and it hurt a lot. I was frustrated that I could not get the first down, and a part of me just wanted to lie there and have the trainer take me off the field. But I remembered Lido's speech about how being a running back is like life and how you always have to be ready to stand back up and move on to the next play. Despite the pain in my leg and my anger from not making the first down, I was able to stand back up.

Coach McDuff decided to kick a field goal, and we made it, which closed our point gap to 8. We needed to stop the Ironmen, get the ball back, score, and make the two-point conversion to tie the game.

Thankfully, our linebacker, Kelly Reynolds, was able to intercept the Ironman pass and we had the ball back with less than 2 minutes left. We were able to drive and Brady hit our tight end Mitch Casey on a 10-yard out pass for the touchdown. We needed a two-point conversion next, and Coach McDuff called my number. He had me do a speed sweep, which was my favorite play. I lined up at slot receiver, went in motion before the ball was snapped, got the handoff when Brady called hike and used my speed to run right around the end. I gave a powerful, stiff arm to the defensive end and sprinted into the end zone to make the two-point conversion to tie the game. Incarnation had one final chance to win, but we stopped them, and the game went into overtime.

During overtime, one team gets the ball and has a chance to score either a field goal or a touchdown, and the other team is on defense. Then, the team on defense gets a chance to play offense and must get more points than the other team to win the game. If they get the same points, it will still be a tie and another overtime.

Incarnation got the ball first, and our defense held them to only a field goal. We only needed a field goal to tie and a touchdown to win. Coach McDuff had an idea to start our drive with a slip-screen pass to me. And you know what? It actually worked. Brady dropped back really far. Our receiver went far down the field as if it was going to be a far pass, and then I slipped out and caught the short screen pass. I had a huge hole, and I ran as fast as possible. The middle linebacker came up to try and tackle me, but I made a great cutback move on him, and he missed me entirely, which caused him to fall to the ground.

After the linebacker was down, the free safety came gunning for my knee, so I jumped over him. I then kept running as fast as I could, and as I jumped into the end zone, the strong safety managed to tackle me and made a hard hit on my injured knee. He was too late because he tackled me into the end zone. The game and season were over! The St. Andrews Americans were the New Jersey Catholic School State Champions!

Our crowd was going wild, and although my knee hurt, I managed to jog off the field excitedly. In my head, I was thinking about all the times I overcame falling down the mountain and how I proved Dr. Horton wrong by playing with a torn ACL all season. Not only did I play all season with a torn ACL, but I helped my team win the State Championship. The stadium blasted "My Champion" by Alter Bridge and "Victory" from *Rocky IV*. I gave Steph, Frankie, Lido, and my parents enormous hugs as our marching band started to play Chicago's classic "Questions 67 and 68," ironically the song I jogged to on the same day I tore my ACL. My dad came over to me and was crying happy tears.

"I am so proud of you son. You were down so many times but you never gave up. You worked harder than anyone ever could. You are a true warrior Drew. I love you so much," he told me with tears running down his face.

I then started crying and told him, "You are the reason I did this. Without your support, training, and courage, I'd still be lying down at the bottom of the hill with an injured knee. I love you so much, Dad," I told him as we both hugged while still crying.

I then found out that I won the 'Player of the Game Award', and because of that, they gave me a microphone and asked me to say a few words.

So I got up, cleared my throat, and stared at the sea of people." Wow. Player of the Game Award in the State Championship. I am so honored to have won this. I've dreamt about winning this award and game my entire life, but there is someone who deserves it more than me.

Lido Jones, I would like you to have this trophy. You have

overcome so many obstacles in your life, and you are so much braver and stronger than I ever could be. He is not just a player of a game but a player of life. He has more determination and drive than anyone I have ever seen. You should see him work out. The last game, I was playing terribly, and he gave me one of the most inspirational speeches anyone has ever given me. He told me how lucky I was to be able to play football and to be able to run, walk and stand. He told me that I had to be ready to stand my ground and never back down. His speech stayed with me all game, and it will stay with me for the rest of my life. So Lido, please take this award."

Everyone started to clap for him. Lido refused to take the trophy at first, but eventually, I convinced him to. The photographers were taking pictures of Lido and me holding the trophy for the newspaper.

Then, I was given the Ironman trophy for playing all season with a torn ACL. Once again, they asked me to say some words.

"Ah, the Ironman trophy. What another honor. Once again, though, someone else deserves this more than I do. I would like to give this to Frankie Rossi. A couple of months ago, there was a tragedy and Frankie was seriously injured. He worked so hard to overcome it and is here today. Although he can't walk now, he is not giving up and we all know that someday he will be ready to stand again. Frankie is way stronger than I could ever be. Both of these men are true heroes. Please give them a round of applause."

The crowd erupted with excitement and were chanting their names. Both Lido and Frankie were in their wheelchairs, holding their trophies high. I couldn't help but get emotional, and I started to cry happy tears. It was one of the most inspirational moments of my life and then something more amazing happened.

First, they chanted "Lido," and then they chanted

"Frankie." As they were chanting Frankie's name, a miracle happened. Frankie handed Lido his trophy for a second and gripped the wheelchair tight. Then he asked me if I could get behind him and hold his chair steady. I then saw the most determined look that I had ever seen on anyone's face. I realized that the crowd and the trophy excited Frankie so much that he was going to attempt to stand in front of thousands of people.

"Here goes nothing." I heard him whisper to himself.

The crowd's cheering got louder and louder and Frankie used every ounce of strength that he had to attempt to stand. The cameraman zoomed in on Frankie and everyone saw him on the video screen. He gripped the wheelchair extremely tight, and got up a tiny bit but fell back down. Then Lido yelled at him to not give up and he went for it again.

Tears were surging down my face, but I couldn't wipe them because my hands were holding Frankie's wheelchair steady. Frankie went for it again, and this time, he stood a little higher but still fell back down.

"Try Again!" yelled Lido.

Once again, Frankie gave everything that he had and got so close but still fell back down.

"Jesus fell 3 times but got back up to save us. Have faith in Jesus. Have faith in yourself!" Lido yelled.

Frankie closed his eyes for a minute and listened as the crowd grew louder than I had ever heard them.

"Ready to Stand!" They were chanting, and Frankie opened his eyes, gripped on tight, dug his feet into the ground, and attempted to stand again. His face looked more determined than ever. He got to the same point as he did the last time. It looked like he was going back down, but he used every ounce of strength he had in him to fight it. I watched slowly as his legs and back straightened all the way.

Frankie actually stood tall while the crowd erupted with excitement! The adrenaline rush and the applause from the crowd, his sheer determination, and his faith in himself and God helped him to accomplish the remarkable feat. He beat the doctor's odds and was standing tall!

The crowd was chanting Frankie and Lido's name again. Frankie picked the Ironman trophy back up and lifted it over his head while still standing. It was the most emotional moment of my life and felt like a scene from a movie. Although Lido had every reason to be jealous that Frankie could stand, he was not at all. He could not have been happier for Frankie. He was truly selfless.

Frankie finally sat down, and I was finally able to wipe away my tears so that I could look like a tough guy again.

I took the microphone back and said, all choked up, "See? That is why those two deserve those awards more than anyone.

"I would also like to thank Coach McDuff for having faith in me and, most of all, my amazing brothers for being my biggest fans, my amazing mother for always taking care of me, my wonderful girlfriend Steph for being my inspiration and always cheering me up when I was down. And finally, my father for being there for me and putting this knee brace together. I wouldn't be here if it weren't for all of you guys. My dad especially never doubted me one second and was with me all the way. Although I never hung out much with my teammates, I love you all. Thank you for coming together as a team at the end and proving that we are the true State Champions." I said with so much passion and intensity. Also thanks to Coach Smith who never had much faith in me but always motivated me to prove him wrong."

Everyone clapped with excitement, even Coach Smith. We were then given our Championship trophy, and our team, Lido and Frankie, all put their hands on it. Our team, Lido and Frankie, were all over the newspaper, the internet, and even ESPN. Frankie's miraculous story of standing in front of everyone and proving the doctor s wrong made national headlines.

It was such a fairy tale ending to a season filled with so many ups and downs. Everything was going well, and the holidays were approaching, but so was my knee surgery that was on December 18th. I was very nervous about it because I had never gotten surgery before. Luckily, Thanksgiving with my family came first before the surgery.

CHAPTER 27: ALL IS RIGHT

After the season, I made third-team All-County, meaning that I was the third-best running back in the county. Although I thought I was the best, my statistics were not the best because I did not get the ball much. Even so, I was still able to run for over 700 yards with a completely torn ACL. I was proud of my season and that I could overcome so much.

The drama finally settled down and I went back to just focusing solely on my beautiful girlfriend Steph, my friends and my family. I also helped Steph train for her upcoming basketball season. She was a talented point guard, and I was excited to watch her play. I was also thrilled to spend my first Thanksgiving with her.

We spent the night before Thanksgiving participating in the Powder Puff football game. Powder Puff football is where senior girls play the junior girls in flag football. I was the Coach, and Steph was the quarterback. She had an amazingly strong arm, and we ended up destroying the juniors in the game. Steph threw for four touchdown passes, and it was so fun watching her compete.

After the game, we watched my favorite Thanksgiving movie, *Addams Family Values,* because I love the whole Thanksgiving play scene. Steph slept over at my house that night, and in the morning, we watched a classic Laurel and Hardy movie, *March of the Wooden Soldiers.* Afterwards, we went to the traditional Thanksgiving high school football game between the Snyder Spartans and the Harrison Hornets.

As I said before, my father went to Snyder, and we had a family tradition of going to the football game every year, except my mom. My mom hated football and only went to watch her sons play. She spent Thanksgiving home cooking and getting ready for the day.

I always loved the Thanksgiving game, but I always wished I could play in it. Despite not missing the drama of football, I still missed playing since my season ended. Before the game, we saw the Stantons. Steve Stanton was PJ's father, and he was my dad's arch-rival in Snyder. PJ was the one who hurt my father's leg. I thought that he should have been suspended for the entire season, but I found out he was only suspended for two games.

I usually rooted for Snyder every year, but because of what Stanton did to my dad, I wanted them to get destroyed. Fortunately for me, they did get destroyed. Harrison dominated them, and we heard Stanton's father screaming at the team and coaches during the entire game.

After the game, we went over to my Grandmom and Pop's house and had a wonderful Thanksgiving with my family. We watched the NFL games together as a family. Usually at Thanksgiving, I never actually took the time to realize what the holiday was really about. I usually would just get caught up in all the football, movies, and delicious food. But that year, I truly felt so thankful that I had such a great family, girlfriend, school year, and football season. I just wished the happy feeling could last forever, but I could sense that rough times were ahead.

CHAPTER 28: BLUES IN THE NIGHT

After Thanksgiving, we went Black Friday shopping at the mall. My father and I split up from Steph and my mom so that we could shop for them. Both my father and I hated shopping, but we wanted to make Steph and my mom's Christmas the best one ever. I had an idea to get Steph an iPod and some jewelry. My dad got my mom a bunch of clothes and jewelry.

Afterward, we met up with Steph and my mom for lunch. Many people noticed me and told me what a big fan they were of mine. It was a great feeling to be recognized, but also a little hard for me because I was very humble and did not like a whole lot of attention drawn to myself.

That Saturday, we had our football awards night. I was honored to receive the Most Valuable Player award and trophy.

Coach McDuff gave me a welcoming smile, as he praised me. "This guy is a true tough guy. Although he lied to me about having a torn ACL, it was for a great reason. He worked so hard in the weight room to prove the doctor wrong, and he won so many games for us. He also had that incredible halftime speech to inspire us to win the State Championship. Please give a hand for our MVP, Drew Russo."

I was so flattered by Coach McDuff's speech, and I received a standing ovation from the crowd. My parents took my family, Steph, and I out to eat afterwards to celebrate.

The next few weeks went by quickly. During the weekend before my surgery, Steph came over to help us decorate and put up the Christmas tree while I played our favorite Chicago Christmas songs such as "Child's Prayer," "Sleigh Ride," "I'm your Santa Claus, "Merry Christmas, I Love you," and many more. I wished I could have frozen time and stayed with my family and

Steph forever in front of the fireplace. The Chicago Christmas song "All is Right" lyrics honestly described my feelings. "We'll all be singing silent night, with a fire so bright, all is right with the world at Christmas time."

My parents then went out to run some errands, so Steph and I had some romantic alone time. We cuddled under the blanket, and I hugged her tight and told her how much I loved her. I also told her how thankful I was to her for being there for me. I just wanted to hug her and hold her in my arms forever. She was the cutest, most beautiful girl, and I was so in love with her. We watched some of our favorite Christmas movies *Home Alone*, *Frosty the Snowman*, and *Rudolph the Red-Nosed Reindeer.* After the movies, another of my favorite Christmas songs came on, "This Christmas." As Chicago's Jason Scheff sang, "And this Christmas will be a very special Christmas for me," I knew that my Christmas would not be one like Jason described because I would be getting knee surgery.

The next day, I returned to Dr. Horton for my pre-operation appointment. I was so nervous, though Dr. Horton congratulated me for proving him wrong.

"Drew, I thought it was impossible. I couldn't believe you did it. We are going to get through this surgery. You're going to be okay," he told me.

I thanked him, and he told me all about the procedure. I was still so nervous, though.

The night before my surgery, Steph slept over because she wanted to help comfort me. I told her that she didn't have to miss school for me, but she said that there was no way that she would be able to focus in school while I was in surgery. She slept on the couch, and I tried my best to sleep in my bed, but I woke up screaming from a nightmare.

In the nightmare, I was still at the top, but the stone was rolling all the way down and pushing me. I was falling, and I woke up in the middle of the night feeling like I was actually falling. I did my infamous high-pitched scream.

When I woke up, Steph asked me what was wrong. She hugged, kissed me and told me everything was going to be okay. I wish I could have believed her, but I just had a bad feeling about the surgery.

The morning of my knee surgery, December 18th, finally came. Chicago's "25 or 6 to 4" was my alarm song that woke me. I was so scared that I started to cry.

"Don't cry, honey. It's going to be alright," Steph said as she hugged me again. My parents came down and hugged me also. I didn't know what I would do if it weren't for them. My dad was also getting his surgery.

"At least we will do this together," my dad told me. He was no stranger to surgery though being that he had so many before.

It was time to get in my parents' van, and Steph sat with me in the backseat. She was hugging me the whole time. We finally arrived at the hospital. It was so hard for my mom because she had both of us to take care of, but it was convenient to do it on the same day. Before we went back, we all hugged each other. My dad hugged me and said how much he loved me. My dad's surgery was a little more severe than mine, but he was not as nervous as I was.

When it was time to leave Steph, I had tears rolling down my eyes.

She kissed me and said, "I love you so much."

I said that I loved her too, and then I had to strip down and put on my hospital gown to lay on the rolling bed. Luckily, my father was close to me. Our beds were rolling right next to each other.

He shook my hand and said, "We are tough and are gonna do this together. I love you son."

"I love you too dad."

Unfortunately, it was time for both of us to go into our rooms for surgery. I started to get choked up as I saw our carts leaving each other. When I got into the room, the doctor had to put me to sleep for the surgery. In reality, anything could have happened, but it was not that serious of a surgery. I was an overdramatic teenager, but I still thought about everything. I had flashbacks of tearing the ACL, rolling the stone of Sisyphus in my dream, kissing Steph, and all of the good and the lousy football games that played. I closed my eyes, and pictured me kissing Steph on the gondola with Chicago's love song "Remember the Feeling" playing in my head as I went fast asleep.

I woke up a few hours later and didn't know where I was at first. Then I saw Steph and my mom in front of me. At first, I forgot what was happening, but then I remembered where I was. I felt like it was only a 10-minute procedure but they told me that I was in there for a couple of hours.

The painkillers were making me overly sweet. I told my mom and Steph that I loved them a thousand times, and they both held each of my hands. The nurse and doctor came, and I told them that I loved them also. They laughed at me because I was so "lovey-dovey." Then they gave me Ginger Ale and Graham crackers. It was delicious, and I had absolutely no pain. It just felt like I took a nice long nap.

Then I remembered that my dad was also in surgery.

"How's daddy?" I asked in a lazy and slow voice.

"He is still in surgery, honey, but he should be out soon," my mom said. "How are you feeling?"

"Great, Mom. I love you both," I told them.

Dr. Horton came back, and I thanked him about 20 times for the surgery. I then looked down and saw my knee with the humungous brace on it. I thought to myself, "Oh no, another knee brace. At least I don't have to play football with this one."

Then another nurse came and asked if I could sign my autograph for her son, who was a big fan.

"Can you sign it to my friend Paulie?" I said yes and signed her autograph.

As she left, I said, "To my friend Paulie, whom I don't even know." It was just like *Rocky II* when he was in the hospital and said the same thing when he was asked to sign an autograph. My mom and Steph laughed because they knew I was doing a Rocky spoof.

Another nurse came in and told my mom that my dad was out of surgery and he was doing great. He said that she could see him.

She turned back to me. "Honey, I'm going to check on Daddy now. I'll be back as soon as I can. Steph's here. I love you guys," she said.

"Love you too," we replied.

My mom left the room, and Steph held my hand.

"I love you so much," she said.

"I love you too."

She then put on the television, and we watched *Seinfeld* and *Friends* together. By then, my painkillers were starting to wear off a little, and I was becoming more myself again. The nurse came in and said that I could go home. They got me into the wheelchair and Steph pushed me out. I saw my mom pushing my dad too. Having both me and my dad on the wheelchairs together reminded me of *Rocky II* when they pushed both Rocky and Apollo on the wheelchairs.

"Hey, Dad. How are you feeling?" I asked.

He said he felt great. My dad started to tell everyone that he loved them, also.

"Was I like this?" I asked, and they nodded that I was.

The nurses helped us get into the car, and my dad and I started singing Chicago's "If This Is Goodbye" as we were leaving the hospital.

When we finally got home, my mom slowly helped my dad in. She laid him on the couch. Then she came out and helped Steph take me into the house. My dad and I were lying next to each other on the couch, and my mom put the television on. We watched sitcoms until it was time for her to go pick my brothers up from school.

My dad had fallen asleep but I had some trouble sitting still so I begged my mom to let me go for the ride. She finally agreed, and Steph helped me stand up. All of a sudden, Steph's face turned white and she screamed.

"What's wrong?" I asked.

She pointed to the ground, and I looked down and saw blood all over the floor. I was in shock, and Steph and my mom were screaming.

"His leg is hemorrhaging. We need to get him to the hospital!"

My dad woke up in a panic. He wished he could come, but he told Steph to get me to the car quickly. Steph and my mom promptly walked me to the car, and my mom rushed me back to the hospital. Luckily, the hospital was only about 8 minutes away from our house. Steph said I looked like Casper the friendly ghost, because I was so pale. She hugged me, held my hand, and told me that I was going to be alright.

Blood was dripping everywhere from my knee. Both my house and my mom's van looked like a murder scene investigation. My mom finally got me to the hospital. She had already called, so the nurses quickly rolled me back in. Dr. Horton came and looked at my knee. I was in so much pain because the painkillers had just worn off, and according to the doctor, somehow, the stitch had popped open.

Unfortunately, he had to stitch my knee back up, and I was losing a lot of blood, so it was an emergency surgery. I could see Steph and my mom's worried faces through the window. The doctor quickly stitched it up, but I was screaming. It was terrible, and a part of me thought that I was going to die. My life was flashing before my eyes, but soon, the blood had stopped. He said that I would be okay and that I actually didn't lose that much blood.

My mom and Steph ran in and told me how much they loved me. They both held my hands again. My dad called my mom to ask how I was. The doctor said it was a freak accident and the stitch popped out, but it was repaired. Although it seemed like I lost a lot of blood, it was actually not that much at all.

"Tell that to my rug and car. I don't care about those things, though. The important thing is that you are okay. I was so worried, Drew," my mom said.

I thanked my mom and Steph for being there for me. I was so relieved that it was all over, but I was still in a lot of pain. Dr. Horton came in and gave me more painkillers. The pain finally started to go away, and they were ready to take me back home. When I got home, I laid back on the couch. Steph ensured I was comfortable, and my brothers came home and hugged me.

Steph helped my mom clean up the blood the best that she could, and then they helped my father go up to bed. Steph stayed over with me to make sure I was alright.

It was so uncomfortable having to sleep with the gigantic knee brace on, and my knee hurt so much. I was crying because I was in so much pain, causing Steph and me to only be able to sleep for about three hours. Our high school was done for winter break so Steph could stay with me all day and night. I felt so bad making her do stuff for me, but she assured me that she liked taking care of me.

I loved working out, so it was hard being housebound and unable to move much. I finally knew what it was like to be in Frankie and Lido's shoes with not being able to walk. The painkillers were able to work most of the time, but sometimes, I would feel a ton of pain. The worst pain came during the night, but Steph was always able to make me feel a little better. It was a very rough week, but luckily, Christmas was coming up, and it was my first Christmas with Steph. I just wished that I could have been able to walk. I knew I would soon be able to stand again.

CHAPTER 29: MERRY CHRISTMAS, I LOVE YOU

Although Christmas was one of my favorite holidays, it wasn't the same since I was on crutches. Still, Steph was able to take me shopping and walking on crutches was actually a good ab workout. Frankie, Lido, Thomas, Allison, and I all went to Winter Wonderland.

Winter Wonderland with my friends was a fun time. In Winter Wonderland, Kuser Park was decorated for Christmas and hosted a grand festival. We had funnel cakes, chicken fingers, and listened to great Christmas carols. I wore my new *Termintator* style leather jacket that my mom bought me as a gift for getting surgery.

When Christmas Eve came, we went to church first. I was looking at the crucifix and trying to find ways to talk to God, but I was still baffled as to why He allowed Frankie to get beaten so badly. I was trying so hard to find my faith again, but I was still struggling.

After church, we went to my dad's parents' house. They had us play a game where we had to go on a scavenger hunt and find different Christmas items in their den. We got our gifts, and my Grandmom and Pop got me the Styx and REO Speedwagon live-in-concert DVD. They also got Steph perfume, and she loved it.

Then Pop called me to his 60s retro-style bar in the den, where he loved to sit, and told me how much he loved Steph. He told me to sit on the bar stool next to him.

"You know, Drew, you are one lucky guy. Steph is one amazing girl, and I know she is perfect for you. You hit the jackpot," he told me and drank some wine afterward.

I smiled, thanked him, and gave him a big hug. I knew that my Pop was getting up there in age, so I cherished every hug and moment I spent with him. After a fun-filled time at Pop's, we went home to get ready for Christmas morning. Steph slept over at our house, and we were so excited to spend our first Christmas together. I wanted to run down the stairs when we woke up, but I still had to crutch my way down. My dad asked my brother to get his video camera because he had to make sure that he videotaped every Christmas and special event so that we could remember them forever.

When I was younger, I would get annoyed by him doing that, but as I got older, I was so grateful that he did because it was awesome seeing my childhood through the years.

First, I opened my gifts from my parents. They got me a new bicep and tricep machine for my attic. I was so excited that I could do an exercise that did not require my legs, as I was not allowed to use my legs yet. They got Steph a nice purse, and she loved it. Then Steph and I took turns opening our gifts for each other. She was so surprised that I got her an iPod, jewelry, and a Chicago the band shirt. She loved all of them.

She got me the Chicago XIV CD, a rare Chicago CD that I didn't have. She also made me a Casper the Friendly Ghost stocking, got me a lot of Ghiradelli chocolate, and gave me some cool Affliction brand shirts. I was excited and happy to spend my first Christmas with the best girlfriend ever.

Later on, we went to my MomMom and PopPop's house with my mom's family next door. My MomMom cooked her traditional pasta dinner and we spent the day in their big basement with family. It was fun, and they were their usual loud Italian selves. It was such an incredible Christmas, and I was so thankful that I had the best family and girlfriend to enjoy it with. I knew that all was right in the world at Christmas time, but I just hoped that things would stay that well in the future.

CHAPTER 30: WISHING YOU WERE HERE

After Christmas, my knee started to improve, and I even started physical therapy. My dad and I went together, and our knees were regaining their range of motion. Although some of the exercises were painful, I was making progress.

But everything changed when Steph had to leave me for three days to visit her aunt in Florida. She didn't want to go, but I wanted her to spend time with her family. I thought I would be okay, but I had no idea how much I would miss her. I was so lonely without her, and all I did was work out my arms with my new bicep and tricep machine.

After my physical therapy appointment, my leg was sore. Although I stopped taking the painkillers for a while, I needed to go back on them to deal with the pain from physical therapy. Sometimes, I felt like my pain was more emotional from missing Steph, and I just wanted to sleep so that my three days without Steph would go by quickly. When I wasn't sleeping, I would do physical therapy exercises for my leg and arm workouts while listening to Chicago's song with the Beach Boys' "Wishing You Were Here." I wanted her to be with me so much, and I just kept wishing she was there like the song said. I knew I loved Steph, but I never realized how much until she left me for those days. Steph told me that she missed me as well, and while she was on the Florida beach with her aunt, she was also listening to "Wishing You Were Here" and thinking of me.

I was in a great depression and my stone had fell down the hill entirely again. My dad had noticed that I had been taking the painkillers and took them away from me because he did not want me to get addicted. I really missed them and would just cry and lay in my bed. I could not sleep because of the uncomfortable brace; all I could think about was Steph. I would play more sad Chicago songs like "A.M. and P.M. Mourning."

I was so pathetic until my dad snapped at me one day. "Drew, I know you miss Steph, but you can't lie here and let this injury kill you. You're being a baby. Wipe off your tears and get back up. I am off my painkillers, and I am doing better than you. I know you can't stand yet, but you must be ready to stand. You have to be ready to go from down to up and be ready to rise above."

My dad's pep talk inspired me to write my all-time best song. I called it "Ready to Stand" because Lido, my dad, and Coach McDuff used that phrase in their speeches. Being ready to stand is also something that running backs have to do on every play. They have to stand back up after getting tackled by the defense. I wanted it to be an upbeat rocker to inspire people, and I wanted it to be a Chicago song someday. A guitar riff popped in my head, and the words and melody just came to me.

"Ready to Stand"

Verse 1:

Another crushing blow

Another all-time low

Another injury

Another blown-out knee

Why is this happening to me

I'm sick and tired of this nonsense

I'm sick and tired of being in this bed

Like a baby learning to walk

Like an accused innocent man who wants to talk

I'm ready to stand

I just need a helping hand

Chorus 1:

I'm ready to go from crawl to creep
I'm ready to awaken from the sleep
I'm ready to learn to run
Under the desert sun
And I'm ready to jump
I'm ready to run through the sand
I'm ready to stand
Verse 2:
Another tragedy to my family
It all happened so suddenly
Another lonely winter
I'm tired of being a loser
It's time to be a winner
Chorus 2:
I'm ready to go from worst to best
I'm ready to pass the test
I'm ready to separate from the rest
I'm ready to learn to swim
In the very deep end
I'm ready to swim my way to land
I'm ready to stand
Bridge:
I just need to put two feet down
Pull myself up and stand my ground
Chorus 3:
I'm ready to go from dark to light

I'm ready to overcome my fright

I'm ready to win this endless fight

I'm ready to rise up from the dead

I'm ready to awaken from my bed

I'm ready to put my faith in God

I'm ready to beat all the odds

I'm ready to always love you

I'm ready to be there for you

Verse 3:

Like a baby learning to walk

Like an accused innocent man who wants to talk

I'm ready to stand

I just need a helping hand

Chorus 4:

I'm ready to go from down to up

I'm ready to rise above

I'm ready to face my fears and be tough

I'm ready to fight the fight with all of my might

I'm ready to win the game and fight through all the pain

I'm ready to fly away and start a brand new day

I'm ready to run through the fire and climb a little higher

I'm ready to save the day

I'm ready to survive the quicksand, and I'm ready to stand

Stand my ground and never back down

It was a song that defined my situation and everyone who has had to overcome adversity, especially Frankie. I had a program on my phone that turned my voice into a guitar, so I made the guitar riff with my voice, sang the melody, and sent it to Chicago's Jason Scheff. He flipped out about it and loved it. He wanted to know if he could sing and play a demo of it so that he could submit it for a Chicago album. I was so excited that Jason would sing and play on the song I wrote. He said it could be the band's hardest rocker since "25 or 6 to 4" from 1970.

I called Steph, told her the amazing news and played her my version of the song. She absolutely loved it, and my parents were really excited too. Everything was going fantastically, and my father and I did awesome in physical therapy. The best news was that Frankie no longer needed to be in the wheelchair. He was officially walking with a cane. All three of us were doing excellent, and I hoped that the next year would be our best year ever.

It was finally New Year's Eve, and Steph was scheduled to be coming home around dinner time. My parents helped me buy some things, and I was going to surprise her with a romantic dinner. Steph and I were so excited to see each other, and I decorated my dining room table with hearts, candles, and flowers. I also bought sparkling cider so that we could celebrate the New Year.

I could not wait to see her beautiful face again. My parents and brothers were going to my aunt's house for a party, but before they left, they had to make sure that I was alright a thousand times. I assured them that I would be fine.

Steph called me and told me that her flight landed and she would be at my house in around an hour. She also said that her phone was dying, so she would have to ring the bell when she arrived. I was listening to my favorite Chicago love songs like "Nothing's Gonna Stop Us Now," "Forever," "Hard Habit to Break," and "I Don't Wanna Live Without Your Love" to get ready to see the love of my life. About an hour passed by, and my doorbell finally rang.

When I heard the doorbell ring, my heart was filled with so much joy that I quickly crutched to the door. I was so anxious to open it and see my beautiful brown-eyed girl. But then my excitement turned into pure shock and fear. I was in shock to see that it was actually Terrance Rex, fresh out of jail, paying me a surprise visit.

"It's payback time, Drew," he said and punched me in the face extremely hard before I could even react.

He just kept punching me, and I was so shocked and injured that I could not defend myself. The constant punching caused me to fall to the ground in agony. I thought that I was going to die without saying goodbye to Steph and my family. There was nobody there but me, and I just wanted him to be gone before Steph got there.

Once again, my life flashed before me, and I didn't know what to do. I just kept thinking about my gorgeous Steph. He must have given me about three blows to my head, and then he was kicking me in the gut. I was bleeding everywhere. A part of me just wanted to give up and die so that he would leave before Steph got there, but then I thought that I could never let Steph find me like that.

I thought about my song "Ready to Stand" and the lyrics. I thought about all of my dad and Lido's speeches. I heard Lido's voice in my head saying "be ready to stand." I thought about rolling the stone back up the hill and Frankie standing up in front of the entire stadium. I knew that I could not give up and let him take away the life that God gave me. But again, I didn't understand why God allowed this to happen. I wanted to die old and gray with Steph and not let that monster take away my life while I was young. I knew that I had to fight back. I knew that Drew Russo always fought back.

I then had an idea to use my good left leg and kick his leg in. I tried it, and I could tell that he was in pain. I saw my crutches on the side, and right as I kicked him, I was able to grab my crutch and hit him extremely hard in the stomach. I was still on the ground, so I took my fist and punched him right in the shin. He was in pain, so he backed away for a moment. I knew I had to stand up and thought of Frankie using every ounce of strength he had to stand. I was finally able to stand, and I just kept delivering blows to his head until he fell.

To be honest, I didn't care if he died at the time because I could not risk him getting to Steph. I punched until he was unresponsive, and then I fell to the ground because I was in so much pain and was so tired from punching. Both T-Rex and I were lying on the ground bloody and beat up. My iPod was still playing, and the song "Savin Me" by Nickelback was blaring from the speaker. As we were lying there, the phone rang, and my dad left a message saying that he had heard from his cop friend that T-Rex was out on bail and that I had to be careful. He said the family was on their way home, but his warning was too late. I could hear what my dad was saying, but my mind was going in and out.

Unfortunately, Steph had to walk in and see me all bloody and in terrible shape. She screamed and quickly ran to me. She kept comforting me, but although I saw her lips moving, I heard nothing.

She quickly called the police and ambulance, and while she was waiting, she got a cloth and was trying to stop the blood on my head. My face was all bloody, but luckily, T-Rex hadn't hurt my injured knee. It was mainly my head, stomach, and ribs. I could tell that my ribs were probably broken. My head was really bad and I was slowly losing consciousness, but I could see T-Rex was getting up. My eyes got huge, and Steph could sense that he was about to attack her. She quickly turned around and punched him, knocking him back down. "Nobody hurts my Drew," she said with so much anger.

"Wow, I wouldn't want to mess with you," I said, barely making out the words with a half-smile.

Steph was smiling, but soon, her smile turned into crying. She hugged me tighter than ever as we waited for the ambulance to arrive.

Although it only took the ambulance about 5 minutes to get there, it felt so long. Ironically, my iPod was still on, and the song "I Just Died in Your Arms Tonight" started to play. I was hoping that I would not actually die in Steph's arms. I didn't want to let Steph go. I was so afraid that T-Rex was going to kill me and that I was never going to see her again. I started to feel sleepy. The last thing that I remembered was falling asleep in Steph's arms. At least, I thought I was asleep...

CHAPTER 31: ALIVE AGAIN

The next thing that I remember was feeling like I was flying away from Steph, who was sobbing, and then seeing all fog around me. I was moving farther and farther from Steph, and she looked microscopic. I could hear Chicago's song "Fancy Colors." Peter Cetera was singing the words, "Going where the orange sun has never died, and your swirling marble eyes shine, laughing, burning blue the light, bittersweet the drops of life, memories only fading." Cetera kept repeating the word "fading," and I felt like my body was lifting in thin air. I suddenly was sitting on a plane in the window seat. I looked out the window and could make out tiny houses.

Then, I heard a gorgeous melody being played on a tin whistle. It was so beautiful and sounded like it could have been a song from the *Titanic* soundtrack. I could not tell where the music was coming from, but it kept getting louder and louder. Then I saw the number of the plane: flight 345. I had been on many planes before, but this plane felt so different. It felt so surreal and peaceful.

Finally, I saw a younger man playing that melody on a tin whistle walking down the aisle. Then, a woman walked by and started singing one of the most beautiful songs I've ever heard. I realized that the woman was actually my Great Aunt Annie, who passed away in the 1970s. She died of heart failure, so I never got to meet her, but I did see many pictures of her at my MomMom's house. For some reason, I noticed her wearing a bracelet with a heart on it.

Between the man's tin whistle and my Great Aunt's gorgeous singing, I was the calmest I'd ever been. I was in complete peace and felt so much love. I looked back out the window, and I could see my life flash before my eyes. The last thing that I remembered was lying in Steph's arms. I missed

Steph, but it felt so incredible on that plane.

Then the plane moved higher. The sky began to get lighter, and soon, I saw a beautiful angel flying outside the plane. The angel was actually my Uncle Nicky, who was my mom's brother, who passed away before I was born. I always wished I could have met Uncle Nicky; he looked exactly how he did in my mom's picture of him in the living room. I knew that I must have been dreaming, but it felt so real. I started to cry, and tears started rolling down my face. I looked outside the window again and wondered if that is what heaven looks like with the clouds and the angels.

I started to cry happy tears because I was so at peace. Suddenly, the cabin light went on, and a thin man with long hair and a beard came and sat next to me.

"Don't cry, Drew," the man said.

"How do you know my name?" I asked him, needing clarification.

"Come on, Drew. You don't know who I am? You pray to me and my Father so much. You and your family worship us a lot, but your dad is always interrupting us with his gagging over the incense," He said with a laugh.

I laughed as well, realizing this man must have been Jesus Christ Himself.

He sighed. "You are a wonderful young man, Drew. You have helped so many people in your young life, but you may want to know that this isn't a dream. You got injured really badly. I'm sorry this has happened to you. But it's not your time to be with me yet. The world needs a man like you in it. You'll have a lot to overcome, and you may be lying in a hospital bed for a while, but you have to be ready to stand again. You have done so many things, but there are many more great things for you to do. I could not be any more prouder of you. You stood by Thomas's side when nobody else in the school would, and you did not care how the other kids treated you because of it. It was just like many people would not accept Me. And how you saved Frankie and your support helped him stand again. You also gave Lido so much inspiration. There are going to be many more people who need your help and many more challenges ahead for you, but you can't give up. I want you to know that my Father and I will always be on your side. So please, when you are lost, look for Our signs; We will help you find your way. My Father and I do not measure people's lives based on how many touchdowns they score or how much money they have. We judge you based on how many people you help. Right now, you are doing an incredible job of helping others. I know you were angry with Me for allowing Frankie to get beat up and for allowing evil in the world. You must know, Drew, that just like you fight evil people like T-Rex, My Father and I also fight evil. Those evil things are the work of Satan getting into peoples' heads. My Father and I try very hard to fight evil, and a lot of times, we do win, but sometimes Satan achieves his goal of getting in their heads just like he did with Adam and Eve. My Father and I love everyone so much, and because of that, we give people the freedom to choose their actions, but sometimes people make the wrong choices and let evil get in their heads. That is why we need people like you on our team down there fighting the evil. We need you to keep helping others in need and spreading Our good word. Love is the basis of everything and you, Drew Russo have so much love in your heart. We need you to spread Our love to others who don't receive love and those who don't know how to love. Now I will let you go so you can have your wedding dance with Steph someday. I will see you again, but not till your life is complete, and you are finished helping others. Keep up the great work, and always be ready to stand when you fall down."

I was stunned. He softly put his hand on my face and wiped my tears again. He then told me to close my eyes. I could hear Celine Dion's "A New Day Has Come" playing.

The last words I heard Jesus say were, "Open your eyes."

When I opened my eyes, I could feel Steph kissing me straight on the lips.

I was lying in a hospital bed surrounded by Steph, my Mom, Dad, brothers, and Dr. They told me that I actually flat-lined and died. Then I went into a coma for 2 hours until Steph kissed me on the lips, and I woke up. I could not believe it, and I started to remember Jesus' words. I knew that I was actually on a plane into heaven, and I had actually just talked to Jesus Christ Himself. I could not tell anyone yet because they would think I was crazy.

"I'm so grateful that you're all here with me. Wait...T-Rex? He did this. Is he in prison?" I asked nervously.

My dad patted my shoulder. "You never have to worry about him again. He's gonna be in prison for a long time. Right now he's in a hospital bed handcuffed because you and Steph beat the crap out of him," my dad said.

Then Thomas and Allison came in and were so happy to see me awake.

Thomas leaned in. "Now that you are better, I can give you something. I found it in the field the other day." He reached in his pocket and took out the cross necklace that I had lost months ago, the night that Frankie was beat up. And suddenly, Jesus' words rang clearer in my mind. I remembered Him saying to look for Their signs.

"The cross is a sign," I said in a low and weak voice.

"What?" My mom and dad asked.

I then decided to tell them about my trip to heaven. I told them about seeing Uncle Nicky and Aunt Annie. I told them how I met Jesus on a plane and what He told me. I told them about my renewed faith and Jesus' encouragement to never give up fighting evil in the world. Finding the cross again must have been a sign that I had newfound faith. Everyone was silent when I was finished, and Steph helped me put my cross necklace on my neck.

At first, it looked like they did not believe me, but then I asked, "Mom, did Aunt Annie always wear that bracelet with a heart on it?"

My mom then broke down crying. "What? Was she wearing that? That was the last gift I ever gave her and the next day she passed. She was not wearing that in any picture and was buried wearing it. There is no way you could have known about that. You must have really gone to heaven. I am so proud of you. Although we were so scared that we were going to lose you, I'm grateful that you finally met my brother, Aunt and that you met our savior, Jesus Christ. Then my brother asked me what it was like to die.

I smiled at him. "It was just like a beautiful and peaceful dream," I told him.

Then, my dad started to apologize. He wished that he could have prevented T-Rex from hurting me. I told him that it wasn't his fault. I was just so lucky to be alive and to be with everyone. I was also happy when both sets of grandparents, Aunts and Uncles, Thomas, Allison, Frankie, and Lido, came to see me. They surprised me with balloons, get-well cards, and chocolate. I was so touched that I was crying happy tears.

In fact, I was swept up by emotion I almost forgot it was midnight. They then put the television on for me so that I could see the ball drop at midnight. At midnight, Steph gave me a kiss and we all said Happy New Year.

Unfortunately, the hospital kicked out everyone a few minutes after the ball dropped because it was hospital rules. Steph hated to leave, but she knew she had no choice.

So once again, she kissed me. "I love you so much, honey. I'll be back soon," she said before leaving.

Once Steph left, I closed my eyes and thought about my past year. I was so proud of myself for overcoming everything, but I knew that the year had already started with me in the hospital. I knew that my stone once again fell all the way back down the mountain, and I would have to fight harder than ever to bring it back up to the top.

I put my headphones on and first played Chicago's rocker "Alive Again" because I literally was alive again. Then I played the very deep Chicago song "(I've Been) Searchin' So Long" because the song was all about finding yourself. The lyrics "When my days have come to an end, I will understand what I left behind, part of me, I've been searchin' so long to find an answer, now I know my life has meaning," really resonated with me because I truly found meaning and faith in my life.

I kept my eyes closed and started to picture heaven. I could hear the melody of the tin whistle playing in my head. Then I opened my eyes when I heard my hospital room door open. A man who looked very familiar came in.

“Hello,” he said kindly. “My name is Timmy. They call me Timmy the Tin Whistler. I play my tin whistle for patients to cheer them up. Would you like me to play for you?"

I was speechless because I thought it was such a coincidence that I had just heard the tin whistle in heaven, but I nodded yes.

He started to play and I got chills when he played the exact melody that the man played on the plane to heaven. I closed my eyes to picture flying with Jesus in heaven, and when I opened them back up, the song stopped, and Timmy was gone. I started to remember the lyrics to the music that my Great Aunt was singing. I quickly paged the nurse so she could give me a notebook to write the lyrics in. She came and gave it to me, and I asked her where Timmy the Tin Whistler went. The nurse looked stunned. She said a candy striper named Timmy worked in the hospital years ago and used to play the tin whistle.

But there is no way he could have been there that night because he passed away about ten years before of cancer. I got chills all over my body when she said that because I knew that a real-life angel was just in my hospital room, and it was another sign from Jesus. The nurse left looking shocked, and I began writing down the song I had heard in heaven.

"Wings in the Sky"

Verse 1:

Sitting on flight 345

Waiting patiently to arrive in Chicago

I listen to soft and slow love songs

I look out and see the clouds

Then, look out and see my tiny house

It feels like I'm leaving the world behind

As I dream about all the ones that I love

And now I'm 30,000 feet above

Chorus:

And all I see are the wings in the sky

I dream I see an angel flying high

I lay there still and softly close my eyes

And think of heaven and suddenly arise to the site of the wings in the sky

Verse 2:

Then I wonder what heaven looks like

I start to think about my late Uncle Mike

Who passed away before I was born

And suddenly I start to feel a little warm

Chorus:

Looking out at the wings in the sky

I dream I see an angel flying high

I lay there still and softly close my eyes

And think of heaven and suddenly arise to the sight of the wings in the sky

Bridge:

Then the sky goes lighter and lighter

The plane moves higher and higher

I start to think about my mother and father, and I start to cry

Chorus:

All I see are the wings in the sky

I dream I see an angel flying high

I lay there still and softly close my eyes and think of heaven and suddenly arise to the site of the wings in the sky

Bridge 2:

Then the cabin light goes on

I start to hear a very pretty song and a voice saying it's not my time to die

I wake up in a hospital bed and realize that I was pronounced dead and on a plane to heaven

But God gave me another chance so I could someday have my wedding dance

But I will always remember that day and cry

That day I saw the wings in the sky

It was such a beautiful song. I couldn't believe that I actually remembered the melody from heaven. Then, all of a sudden, I heard the back door of my room open. I thought it would be a doctor or maybe even another angel, but to my surprise, it was Steph.

"Shhh," she whispered, quite loudly in fact. "I snuck in."

"Steph...you're gonna get in trouble. Where are you going to sleep?"

"The chair right next to you," she said sarcastically.

I couldn't help but laugh. I then sang her the song that I heard in heaven. She said it was gorgeous and I also told her about Timmy the Tin Whistler and how he came to visit me. Steph believed me. Then I got another great idea for a song that I wanted to call "True Love's Kiss." Her kissing me awake reminded me of all of those Disney fairy tales because her true love's kiss literally woke me up. I turned the page, and with help from Steph, I started to write:

"True Love's Kiss"

Verse 1:

I kissed so many girls before

But all of them left me wanting more

I could never find that Mrs. Right

Until that one enchanted night

When you came to me so suddenly and we shared are true love's kiss

Chorus:

Woah, woah, woah

I got chills when our eyes locked across the room

I knew I had to go up to you very soon

Before I knew it

We were outside under the moon

Feeling so much bliss

I knew it was true love's kiss

Verse 2:

I couldn't believe it all happened so fast

It really made me forget about the past

I could feel that this magic would always last

When we shared our true love's kiss

Chorus 2:

Woah, woah, woah

I got chills when I found you my princess

You looked so stunning in that lovely white dress

Before I met you, my life was one big mess

And now I'm all alone with you, feeling all the bliss of our true love's kiss

Bridge:

Your kiss made me awaken from my bed

Your kiss made me rise up from the dead

Your kiss is all I wanted and more

Winning you gave me a perfect score

Chorus 3:

Woah, woah, woah

I got chills when I married you on the beach

I can't bear to have you out of my reach

I got chills when I said I do cause I knew that my life with you was so true

I got chills when I said my wedding vows

We are not only lovers but also the best of pals

Together forever feeling all the bliss of our true love's kiss

After the most dramatic moment of my life and writing two pretty songs that described them, I was finally getting sleepy. I kissed Steph goodnight, and we both fell asleep. I woke up the next morning to Steph sitting over me and just smiling.

“I love watching you sleep. You're so cute," she said.

Then we heard the doctor coming, and she quickly hid in the back room. He came in to check on me, and when he left, Steph promptly came back in. She said that she was going to sneak out. I told to be careful.

Later that day, I was in a lot of pain. Between, my ribs, my head, and my newly repaired ACL, I didn’t know where to begin and I had to go back on the pain killers. But I also got a phone call from a ton of reporters who wanted to interview me about what happened with T-Rex.

At first, I thought about not telling anyone that I saw heaven, but then I remembered to be true to myself and God. Even if people thought that I was crazy, I had strong faith. I knew that Jesus wanted me to spread His word. I actually saw Jesus Himself, and I needed to share that with the world. So when the reporters came, I described the entire night and how I thought T-Rex was Steph. I explained how he punched me when I opened the door. I described the details of the fight and how I fell asleep in Steph's arms. And finally, I described Heaven.

The next day, my story made national headlines. The title was "Football Hero Visits End Zone in Heaven." It was a wonderful article, but many people did not believe that I actually saw heaven. The internet was filled with doubters, but I expected that. Many people still even doubt that Jesus rose from the dead.

That weekend, Father Stan asked me to give a speech at

the end of Mass, but only if I was up for it. He wanted me to tell my story of seeing heaven to the Parish Community. Although a part of me did not feel like standing in front of the Church on crutches, I knew that I needed to do it. I needed to spread the word of the Lord. I remembered what Jesus told me about how He and His Father would measure our lives with how much we help people. I had true first-hand proof that Jesus was indeed real and that we would all join Him in heaven one day. I also broke down some more lyrics from some of my favorite Chicago songs that inspired me. In the song "I Stand Up," Chicago's Robert Lamm sang "You'll never lose me to temptation, fighting the devil and I beat the dragon too. I'm at your rescue; I'm your faithful one. I stand up, believe in myself, If you love somebody stand." This song was all about fighting temptation and being there for people you love and it inspired the speech that I was going to give during mass.

A few days later, it was time to give my speech. I crutched my way up, stared at the crowd, took a deep breath, and began. "How many of you have ever doubted God in the face of tragedy?"

Although some people hesitated initially, the entire mass eventually raised their hands, myself included. I gave them a reassuring smile.

"Don't be guilty, guys. A few months ago, a great friend of mine and one of the nicest people ever was severely beaten up and wasn't able to walk for a long time. I was devastated. I couldn't understand why it happened. I asked myself over and over. Why did God allow this to happen? Why does God allow tragedies like September 11th to happen? I was so angry, and I went to my high school and did workouts all night to release my anger. You see this cross I wear on my neck? I've been wearing this for years, and on that night, I lost my cross necklace. I also lost much of my faith in God.

But some things happened to my friends and me after

that. My friend Frankie miraculously was able to stand after we won the State Championship in a stadium filled with over 1,000 people. Then, I had knee surgery and ended up hemorrhaging. On New Year's Eve, I was attacked by the same guy who attacked my friend, and I ended up dying in my girlfriend's arms for a few minutes. Some of you do not believe me, but it is true. I was on a plane ride to heaven. I saw angels, heard gorgeous music, and saw a couple of my relatives who had passed away.

Then all of a sudden, Jesus sat next to me. He said He was proud of me for helping so many people, and He knew I was angry that my friend was beaten up. He told me He needs people like us to spread faith and love. Love is the most important thing in the world and universe. Jesus said that the evil stuff that happens on earth is the work of Satan corrupting people. Satan tricks people still today just like he did with Adam and Eve. He told me that He and His Father try to fight Satan just like we fight him and his temptations. A lot of times, good prevails, but sometimes Satan has the last laugh, and some tragic things happen because of his work.

Jesus said He gives people free will because he loves us, but sometimes people choose evil. He told me He needs good people like us to fight on his team. Jesus told me that it was not my time to die yet and to look for His signs. He needs us all to fight the good fight to defeat the evil Satan. We all have to convince people to do the good work of God and not the evil work of Satan. We can all defeat evil by love. Evil does not stand a chance against us if we have enough love for everyone.

After my girlfriend Steph woke me up with true love's kiss, my friend brought me the cross necklace I lost that night. It was a sign that my faith was finally back. My plane ride to heaven was a once-in-a-lifetime experience for me. Although I was dead for a few minutes, it was not scary at all. It was so peaceful and surreal. Although most of you may only get to meet Jesus when you pass, you still have to believe He is always with you, no matter what. I know things happen that we don't understand, but we cannot keep letting evil beat us.

Like the Greek myth of Sisyphus, we are all trying to push the stone up to the top of the mountain, but there is always Satan on the other side trying to push it back down. But we cannot give up and let Satan beat us. We have to be there to push it back up. Every single day is like a new game, and we have to live every day to the fullest and be the best people we can be. I know that if we keep spreading the word of God, we can defeat evil. There will be some tragedies that will happen, but we can never give up when we lose. We have to hold each other's hands, wear our crosses, believe, have faith, and be ready to stand up for our Christian faith every single day. Because at the end of the darkest tunnel, the beautiful light of heaven will be waiting for us. I know for a fact it is there. No matter how dark our lives may seem, that light of heaven will always be there. So now, please all hold each other's hands. On the count of 3, stand up and say, I will be ready to stand up for my faith every day, and even if I lose, I will never give up."

I looked and saw a choir of happy tears. Everyone looked so inspired and it really seemed as if I got through to them. I counted to 3, and the entire church stood in unity and declared their faith. It was another incredible moment to see the whole church stand at once and have so much faith and determination. Everyone stood and said those words with so much conviction.

When it was over, so many people thanked me for changing their lives. When we left church, I saw a plane flying over us. I knew that it was another sign from God and that it must have been the wings in the sky in heaven.

That night, they announced that T-Rex was out of the hospital and locked away in jail. I knew that we were all finally safe from him, although I still prayed that we would one day find the other man that beat up Frankie. I was able to go back to physical therapy and worked on getting my strength back. I had to overcome the torn ACL, and I had to overcome the injuries that T-Rex gave me. I knew my work was cut out for me, but I felt higher than ever. I knew there would be nothing that I wouldn't be able to handle because of how much I had overcome already.

I finally got back to school, but I was still on crutches and had a bandage on my head. I was all beat up, but my fellow students treated me with so much respect. So many people volunteered to help me carry my books and were willing to do anything for me. It was also time to think about college and unfortunately, none of the Division I or Division II teams wanted me mainly because I tore my ACL. A torn ACL often can ruin a running back's career, and many colleges did not want to take a chance on me. I didn't get scholarship offers despite all of the media attention that I received. I knew I wanted to play college football, but my dad wanted me to take a year off to rehab my knee adequately.

So I decided to go to community college first to take a year off from football to properly rehab my knee. Although college was just around the corner, I wasn't ready to think about it yet. I still had a long road to recovery and had something else to prepare for: the Sunlight Classic All-Star Game.

Coach McDuff called me in his office one day and asked how my rehab was going. He told me that I made the Sunlight Classic All-Star Game. He said he knew that I had a lot of rehab to do so if I wasn't ready not to worry. But I told him that I had been going to that game since I was a little kid with my dad, and I had always dreamt of playing in it. I was ecstatic when he told me that I had made the All-Star team, and I told him that it was a dream come true. I assured him that I would do whatever it took to overcome my injuries and be ready for that game.

More exciting news came later when I got home and checked my email. There was an email from Chicago's Jason Scheff.

It read, "Drew, Chicago really loved your song "Ready to

Stand," so we put together a demo for it. This is just a rough demo, but I wanted you to have it. It has a great chance of making the next Chicago album! You're a great songwriter! Keep on writing."

It was one of the most beautiful messages that I had ever received. Jason sent the song as an attachment, and when I opened it, I was blown away.

It started with Keith Howland playing the rocking guitar riff that I wrote, then the classic Chicago horns came in and Jason's soaring tenor voice was actually singing my song. Hearing Chicago sing my story about overcoming my obstacles was the most incredible feeling. It was two dreams coming true on the same day: Getting picked for the Sunlight Classic Game and Chicago singing a song that I wrote. That song soon became my new theme song and workout song. It was incredible and that night it inspired my dad and I to work out. We worked out as hard as we could listening to my song as well as Chicago's classic anthem "Feelin' Stronger Every Day." The lyrics of "Feelin' Stronger Everyday" were "I do believe in you and I know you believe in me." My dad and I both believed in each other so much. We felt ready to stand, and we were feelin' stronger every day.

Everyone could relate to my song, and it could motivate anyone. I hoped it would one day be a stadium sports anthem like Survivor's "Eye of the Tiger." Steph, who was currently having a stellar basketball season, was also motivated by the song.

The next day, I went to watch her play basketball, and she had her all-time best game. I wore her away jersey just like she wore mine, and I was her biggest cheerleader. She scored 24 points and had 11 assists in the game. She led the team to a victory, and they ended up getting first place in their division.

I was so proud of her and kissed her after the game. Unfortunately, Steph was too small, and no colleges wanted her for basketball, just like no colleges wanted me for football. Steph really wanted to go to college with me, but she had gotten an academic scholarship to Grant University and she couldn't turn it down.

After I went to community college, I wanted to walk on to St. Thomas in Philadelpha's football team. I knew I could make the St. Thomas football team, even though it was a Division I school, but my knee needed to be 100 percent. My father believed that taking a year off would allow me to return to 100 percent.

It stunk that Steph and I were going to different colleges. We were really going to miss each and wanted to cherish each moment that we had with each other before college. Our first Valentine's Day was also coming up and I had some plans to make it extra special for her.

CHAPTER 32: JUST YOU N' ME

Valentine's Day had finally come. My MomMom and PopPop were spending the night in Atlantic City, so my mom let Steph and I spend the night at their house for some romantic alone time. Steph knew that we were going to go there, but she did not know what I was planning on doing. When she got home from basketball practice, I anxiously waited for her at my MomMom's house door. She parked, got out, kissed me, and walked in.

She was shocked to see MomMom's house all decorated with roses, balloons, and Valentine's Day decorations. I had also ordered Chinese food and had it set up at the table.

I had the music remote in my hand, and I clicked it to start playing a beautiful melody. I then started singing the song I wrote for her, "Paradise in Your Eyes."

I sang the lyrics, "I was so lost for most of my life, but ever since I met you, everything feels so right, I promise to always be by your side, cause everytime I look at you, I always see paradise in your eyes."

She smiled bigger than I ever saw her smile before. When I finally finished the song, she hugged and kissed me more than ever.

"You never cease to amaze me, Drew Russo. Even on crutches, you're still my knight in shining armor. I had no idea all of this was going to happen. I have a surprise for you, too," she said.

Then she started playing my MomMom's piano and sang a song that she wrote me for called "My Valentine." I was so surprised and touched that I had tears in my eyes because I had never heard her sing. I did not even know that she could play piano. The lyrics that she wrote were beautiful.

"My Valentine"

Verse 1:

Time goes by so fast

I know that things don't last

But we have to cherish everything

And now is the time to sing

Chorus 1:

I'll always love you darling

I'll always be there for you baby

I know that you're my Valentine

I wanna be yours 'til the end of time

Verse 2:

I don't need no roses

I don't need no Cupid

I just need your kisses

I wanna be your Mrs.

Chorus 2:

You are my knight in shining armor

And my hero now and forever

I know that you're my Valentine

I wanna be yours 'til the end of time

Verse 3:

You'll always be my only man

I want you to hold my hand

As we walk through the sands of time

I want you to be forever mine

I told her how much I loved it, and we kissed again. After our delicious Chinese dinner, we had the difficult task of finding a movie to watch. We raided my PopPop's videos and found a few classic Abbot and Costello movies. We watched *Abbot and Costello Meet Frankenstein* first and laughed so hard.

We then watched one of our favorite Disney movies, *The Lion King*. We hadn't watched it in a few years, but it brought back childhood memories. We were really corny and even sang along to the music written by Sir Elton John. Because my grandparents had two chairs in front of their television spread apart, we decided to cuddle on the ground with pillows and blankets.

After the movies, I put on a new radio station that I found called Radio Crème Brulee. Steph was wondering why we were listening to it but then she heard my voice come on the radio.

"My name is Drew Russo and I would like to dedicate the song "Just You N' Me" by Chicago to my beautiful and amazing girlfriend Steph Marino. Steph, this past year has been the best year of my life with you. You truly are the love of my life and my inspiration. I love you so much."

Then Chicago's classic love song "Just You N' Me" started to play. It was one of our theme songs because she truly was the love of my life and inspiration. It was one of our most romantic nights ever. Things were definitely looking up for me. I just had to keep them that way.

CHAPTER 33: ONCE IN A LIFETIME

After our wonderful Valentine's Day, I had an appointment with Dr. Horton so that he could see how my knee was healing. He said that it was looking good but that it was still a little swollen. He had to stick a needle in it and drain more blood. Luckily, Steph was with me, holding my hand. After they drained the blood, he said my knee should start to regain its range of motion. He said that I would actually be ready to stand and walk without crutches in two weeks.

The Doctor said it was time for me to stand two weeks later. He took the crutches from me and said, "Alright, Drew, bear weight. Are you ready to stand?" He asked, and I had been ready for so long.

So I slowly put my feet down and stood up again for the first time in so long. It felt amazing!

Then he said, "Alright, Drew, it's time to walk. It's going to be awkward at first, but just take one step at a time."

Slowly, I took one step at a time, and soon I was walking. The Doctor told me not to overdo it, and Steph said that she would make sure that I would not overdo it. Physical therapy was going wonderful and they had me doing exercises to strengthen my legs. Unfortunately, I lost a tremendous amount of muscle mass in my legs, but I knew that with hard work, I could get them back. I was also still going to the community center with Steph to train the people with paraplegia. Everything was going fantastic, and my grades in school were better than ever. I got straight A's for the first time in high school.

Finally, May came, and it was time for our family vacation in Orlando, Florida. We always went to Orlando and that year we went to Disney World and Universal Studios. Of course, Steph came with us, and it was one of the best trips. I am a little embarrassed to admit it, but I was afraid to go on roller coasters and high-drop rides. Steph loved them, though, so she went with my brothers and dad. My mom was afraid like me so she and I sat and ate fruit as we watched and video-taped them. My dad, Steph, and brothers made fun of me because I was afraid, but I didn't care. I overcame a lot of fears but I wasn't ready to overcome that one.

Family vacations were important for my family because we loved spending quality time together. Honestly, I always took my family for granted until my rough year. Before that, I was so shallow. I only really thought about football, working out, pretty girls, and Chicago, but after that past year, I started thinking more about cherishing every moment with my loved ones, especially since I died and came back. We had so much fun in Disney World, and I went on some of my favorite rides, such as Pirates of the Caribbean and The Haunted Mansion.

The best part of the vacation came when Chicago played a free concert in Universal Studios. Thanks to Jason, we had front-row seats. Before the band came out, they played a Chicago medley on the speakers of some of their greatest songs, such as "Once in a Lifetime," "Only You," "You're Not Alone," "If She Would Have Been Faithful..." and many others.

Then Chicago came out and opened up with "Dialogue Parts 1 and 2," "We Can Stop the Hurtin" and "Along Comes a Woman." They then said they were doing a new song that would be on their new album.

Jason smiled and said, "I would like to call out someone from the stands to rock out with us. Please welcome the writer of this song and the guy who played an entire football season with a torn ACL. He also helped his high school win the State Championship. Please welcome my friend and workout buddy, Drew Russo."

I was in total shock and so was my family. My idol actually

called me up on the stage and gave me a guitar. When I hurriedly turned to him, he simply whispered to just pretend to play. Keith started the riff of "Ready to Stand" and Jason and I ran over to him. All three of his were lined up shoulder to shoulder with our guitars playing the riff that I wrote while doing a little dance.

Then, Jimmy Pankow, Walter Parazaider, and Lee Loughnane's horns started kicking in, and were dancing around us. It was surreal that I was actually on stage with my favorite band in the world fake playing a song that I wrote. The crowd was going wild and Jason was singing it amazingly. I was jumping up and down with the guitar while headbanging and my parents were loving it. I had never seen my family and Steph get so excited. Keith Howland then performed a shredding guitar solo.

Soon, the song was ready to end so Jason and I ran to the edge of the stage and did a massive jump with our guitars to end the song. It was the best experience ever. I went back down, and everyone hugged me. It was definitely another one of the best nights and vacations. Like the 80s Chicago song said, it was a "Once in a Lifetime" experience.

CHAPTER 34: I STAND UP

When I got home from my fairy tale trip, Dr. Horton finally allowed me to start running, but there were some restrictions.

"I'm gonna let you run, but only a few times a week and extremely slow. If you sprint or go too fast you'll end up damaging your knee again."

Although I hated that I couldn't sprint, I knew I had to follow the Doctor's orders. I knew that I was lucky even to be alive, let alone be able to sprint.

I initially ran only two laps, then gradually increased it to a mile and a half between the two weeks. When I returned to Dr. Horton, I was so excited because he allowed me to start sprinting a little and lift light weights with my legs again.

My dad and Steph took me to the track, and my dad slowly had me doing sprints. I wanted him to time me in the 40-yard dash and at first he was hesitant because I had not sprinted hard in months. I begged and begged him until he said yes.

Before he timed me, I did a few half-speed sprints and worked my way up. I told him that I was finally ready to get timed. I got down in my stance and exploded off the line. My leg felt good, but I wasn't used to sprinting.

When I reached the finish line, I asked my dad for my time, and he told me it was 4.8. I was surprised and furious.

"What? Are you kidding? I was running 4.5 last year!" I was angry, and he could tell.

"Drew, you need to settle down. Your body just isn't used to sprinting. I guarantee you that you'll be down to 4.5 in two or three weeks."

I disagreed and thought that I lost my speed because of my surgery.

My dad was right like always because in 3 weeks, I wasn't running a 4.5, but even better. I was actually running 4.45 seconds in a 40-yard dash. I was so happy with how I overcame my surgery, hemorrhaging, coming back from the dead and I still became faster than I ever was.

Football wasn't the only thing on my mind, though. We had the court case for T- Rex. Luckily, he was put away for many years for beating up Frankie and attempting to kill me. It was so hard looking at him sitting there with a smug look on his face. He did not even look sorry for what he had done. He kept giving me dirty looks like he still wanted to kill me. I did have mixed feelings, though, because after meeting Jesus, a part of me thought that T-Rex was just an ordinary man who gave into temptation by the devil. Although I was happy that he was taken away in handcuffs for a long time, I prayed that he would find God someday.

After the court case, Steph and I drove to Long Beach Island to relieve some of that stress. Unfortunately, once we got there, we found out that my beloved Pop was rushed to the hospital. He was very sick, and the doctors didn't know what was wrong with him at first. He was 82 years old, but it was hard to hear that he was ill. When we heard that he was in the hospital, Steph and I quickly rushed there to see him.

Eventually, they managed to get him stable and he was doing a little better. My Grandmom and Aunt Janet were also there. Pop then signaled for me. He couldn't talk loud, but I could still hear him.

"Drew, I am so proud of the man that you have become. You were faced with so much adversity this past year and seeing you overcome that is what makes me want to overcome mine. But the truth is I am an old man, and my time is running out. I will fight as hard as possible, but if I don't make it, I want you to know I love you so much. Seeing your interviews, reading your articles, watching you help people and overcome everything... makes me so proud of you. You are a great grandson and man. You telling me that you met Jesus in heaven also gives me so much hope and so much to look forward to," he said in a weak and tired voice.

I tried so hard not to cry, but I couldn't help it. I was sobbing.

"Pop, I love you so much. That meant everything to me. You are my hero, and I don't care how old you are. You're going to overcome this. We'll be there for you. Hey, I have a Sunlight Classic game soon. You have to watch it on television," I told him as tears poured down my eyes.

He grabbed my hand tight. "Goose, I promise you that I will stay alive to watch you kick butt in the game."

He called me Goose because that was his nickname for me sometimes.

Then he turned to Steph. "Steph, you make my grandson so happy. You are truly a very wonderful and special girl. I am so glad that I got to know you. I love you like you were my own granddaughter."

By the time he finished, Steph was sobbing, but he grabbed her hand and kissed it. We both hugged him so tight as if it could be the last time we might ever hug him.

A few moments later, the Doctor came in. He said that he was doing much better, but it was late, and we had to let him rest. Grandmom decided to take Steph and me out for ice cream. Despite her worries, we had a lovely time with her.

After ice cream, we slept over at Grandmom's shore house. The next day, they said that Pop was hanging in there. We went home after we went to the beach because I had a meeting for the Sunlight Classic game. We said goodbye to Pop, and I thought he would make a complete turnaround. He did not look great but he did not look like a man that was dying. I did believe that God would look over Pop and be with him all the way.

Both East and West teams were present at the Sunlight Classic Meeting. I was on the West team, and we were playing the East team. Unfortunately, both PJ Stanton and Shane Hitt were on the East team. Seeing them there really made me angry, and of course, after the meeting, they started talking trash.

"Hey Drew, you are going down this game. We're gonna finish what T-Rex started." Stanton said.

I stood tall and spoke, "Just so you know Stanton, Steph and I took care of T-Rex and if you mess with me, I'll take care of you too."

I usually did not talk trash, but I couldn't believe they had the nerve to bring that up. T-Rex literally killed me, and they were actually rubbing it in my face. Not only that but I beat them both and won a State Championship with a torn ACL.

Although many people thought that the All-Star game was just for fun, it wasn't for Stanton, Hitt and me. They wanted to team up and get revenge on me, and I wanted to stay on top. This was war for us. I walked away and when I got to my jeep, I realized that they slashed my tires. I had to call my dad to come and pick me up.

After that, I was even more furious with them. I worked out harder than ever up in the attic with my dad blasting "Burning Heart" and "Hearts on Fire" from *Rocky IV* soundtrack and Chicago's rocker "Hearts in Trouble." I also listened to Chicago's Stone of Sisyphus" again, and the lyrics "I'm gonna take the Stone of Sisyphus, I'm gonna roll it back to you, wall of stone around the two of us, that only angels can break through." Those lyrics made more sense to me. I needed to push my stone all the way up and build a wall that only angels and good could penetrate. I actually met real angels, and I needed to use my good to beat my 2 opponents who let evil get into their heads.

I wasn't going to let my two enemies beat me in front of everyone. I knew they might try cheap shots, but I didn't care. My leg felt great, my ribs felt great, my head felt great, and I was faster than ever. I couldn't wait for the game, but I knew our high school graduation ceremonies would have to come first.

CHAPTER 35: IF THIS IS GOODBYE

Our graduation was a momentous turning point in our lives. It meant that we were no longer kids, and my mom was taking it really hard by crying all the time that her firstborn was growing up. The hardest part was that I was attending a college different from Steph's. Steph got accepted to Grant University in North Jersey, and I was staying at my hometown community college to give my knee a chance to heal fully.

On the other hand, Thomas got accepted into the University of Penn. Allison was going to the same college as Steph and would be a cheerleader. I was jealous that Allison got to go to the same college as Steph. Although I was excited to see what college was like, some of me didn't want to grow up. I hated change and loved my life the way it was, but I knew it was time to move on.

On our graduation day, everyone was filled with sadness and excitement. Thomas Simmons was the Valedictorian of the school. That meant he had the highest academic achievements in the class and had to give a speech in front of everyone. I could tell how nervous Thomas was. I asked him if it was mandatory to provide the speech, and he said he could have passed, but he wanted to conquer his fear. He told me that he had been going to a special public speaking teacher, and he felt like he was ready. I gave him some words of encouragement and told him how proud I was to be his friend. Allison also told him how proud she was of him.

He slowly walked up when they called him up to the stand in front of thousands of people.

Thomas looked around for a moment and then started to speak. "If you would have told me last year that I would've given a speech to my entire class and their families at graduation, I would have told you that you were crazy. I would've never done it, but I changed now. I mean, let's be honest. I'm a nerd, and up until last year, many of you picked on me, didn't talk to me, didn't know who I was, or thought my name was Timothy. And maybe I deserved it. I was socially awkward. But it prepared me for the real world. It pushed me to work hard in school because I knew I did not have much of a social life.

For the first three years, only one man accepted me. He didn't care that I was a dork and that talking and sitting with me would cause him to lose friends. I needed a friend, and he didn't care that he was a star football player; it made him look horrible in front of the cool kids. He stood up for me and became my friend. Then, I got to know my girlfriend, who would also become my best friend. So yeah, I did suffer a lot. But you know what? Those experiences made me confident in myself. It made me a stronger person. Although my high school memories weren't great during my first three years, my last year was amazing.

So now that we enter college, we're going to have to make some more big changes. Some of you will go to huge schools, and some might get lost in the pack. I hate to say this, but some of you might even get picked on like I used to but don't let that intimidate you. You are ready to overcome any obstacle in your way in college. I hope you meet a Drew Russo, Steph Marino, and Allison Hanson, who are there for you as I did. I hope you all can see people for who they are inside and not just their exterior. I wish you all the best. Although I have never talked to some of you, you are all my St. Andrew's brothers and sisters. God Bless you all."

Thomas' speech brought tears to everyone's eyes, especially mine. Soon, I had to follow his speech because I had been voted the most popular kid in the class, meaning I had to give the speech.

I was really nervous, but I had also been practicing and

was as ready as ever. I slowly walked up to the stage and stared at the sea of people. If I could play football in front of them, I should be able to speak in front of them. I took a deep breath and started.

"Wow. I'm not gonna lie. I'm really nervous. I'm used to playing football in front of many people, but I wear a helmet to hide my face. Thomas's speech was so touching, but I was in the same boat as him. If you had told me last year that I would be up here as the most popular guy in the class, I would have thought it was a prank. I was so shy. I'm still so shy. But after everything that's happened, I am talking in front of thousands of people. I have really come a long way.

And, like Thomas, my first three years weren't great, but this last school year has been magical. You guys truly were always there for me when I was in need, and I can't thank you enough. You were there for me when I had knee surgery, when I died and came back, and every time I needed you, the entire student body was willing to help. We made so many memories, and I will never forget you. And again, as Thomas said, college will be a considerable change. Many of us are going to have ups and downs. You know, ever since I tore my ACL last year, I have been getting recurring dreams of rolling a large stone up a vast mountain. It was weird because I would push the stone up to the top when good things happened to me. The stone would fall on the days that bad things happened, and I would have to push it back up.

Mr. Stevens talked about the Greek Myth of Sisyphus. That summed up my last year. It was a roller coaster ride full of ups and downs, but that is what life is. I hate to say this for those who haven't fallen yet, but you will fall at one point. Everyone in the world will fall at least a few times in their lifetimes. College is going to be so much more challenging. And as we get older, we are going to fail much more. But we can't ever give up. Sometimes, it will feel like we want to lie in bed and give up, but we can't. We need to keep fighting, stand, and keep rolling that stone back up. I love people so much, and we all go through rough times. I promise that even though I haven't personally talked to many of you, we're still classmates, and I promise to be there for any of you like all of you guys were there for me at the end.

I also learned that everyone has a different situation in life. I thought my life was hard until I started training people with paraplegia. I ended up becoming great friends with a boy named Lido. Lido told me that he wished that he could play football and that he could walk. He told me I didn't realize how lucky I was to have gone to such a great high school and to have parents who paid our tuition. How fortunate I was to have two working legs. We will all face many obstacles, but we must be ready to overcome whatever stands in our way. We have to be ready to stand."

I then read the lyrics to my song "Ready to Stand."

I looked up and said, "We all must be ready to stand our ground and never back down. We need to fight for our goals and dreams. We all have dreams; now is our chance to use our God-given talents to help people accomplish their dreams. Don't let fear stop you. Fear is something that kills dreams, but you have to overcome your fears. Sometimes, we may feel like garbage and that our dreams will never come true, but we can't give up. If you can't do it alone, you must reach out for a helping hand. Like the Chicago song "Stone of Sisyphus" says, dreams are make-believe until blood, sweat, and tears turn faith to will."

You need to stop fantasizing about your dreams and do whatever it takes to achieve them. Don't say that you will achieve your dreams a year from now or five years from now. Achieve them now. You are all my brothers and sisters, and I will always love and be there for any of my fellow St. Andrew's class. I love you all and God Bless you!"

After the ceremony, everyone was congratulating me

and Thomas. I only hoped that I inspired some people. My parents and Steph's parents threw us a joint party to celebrate graduating at The Roman Hall in Chambersburg. We had our private room, and both of our families came. My entire immediate family came except for my Grandmom and Pop because Pop was still in the hospital. It hurt not having them there. Even so, it was still a great party with fantastic food and music. I was the DJ and played all my favorite Chicago songs and oldies, especially Chicago's "Old Days" and "If This Is Goodbye," as I thought about some of my old days in high school.

After the party, my dad drove us to see Grandmom and Pop. Pop wasn't doing too good, and although I did not want to admit it, I knew he would pass away very soon. But when I saw him, he was awake. I told him how much I missed him and Grandmom at the party. He said he missed me too, but he looked so weak. He wished me luck on the Sunlight Classic practice and said he couldn't wait to watch me on television.

"Karate Kid, I need to tell you something." He also called me Karate Kid because he thought I looked like young Ralph Macchio.

"I am not doing well, and my time is running out. I had a great life. I want to see your Sunlight Classic Game first before I pass on. I will do whatever it takes to fight to watch you."

I had tears in my eyes. "Pop, thank you so much. The good news is that I've been to heaven, and it is absolutely amazing. I will see you again one day, I know it. I love you so much, Pop," I told him while crying.

We spent about 2 hours with Pop and Grandmom, and it was great to bond with them. We eventually had to leave, and I hugged them both tightly, and they told me how much they loved me. As sad as it was that I knew I might never see Pop in person again, I knew for a fact that I would see him again in the most peaceful setting ever: heaven. I was inspired to win the Sunlight Classic Game and play my absolute best just for Pop.

I loved him so much and wanted one of his last memories on earth to be of me, making him even more proud.

CHAPTER 36: FOR THE LOVE

I showed up for my first day of practice for the Sunlight Classic, and my dad and Steph were watching me on the bleachers. On the first day, we just wore helmets, shoulder pads, and shorts. My knee felt spectacular, and I felt faster than ever. I still wore my cumbersome brace to protect my knee, but I was running great. It felt incredible to be amongst the best players in the county. My fellow teammates were kind to me and treated me with much respect, as did the head coach.

After practice, I drove Steph down to LBI to see Pop and Grandmom again. Pop was still slipping but was ecstatic to see me. After spending a couple of hours with them, we drove to the beach and had a really romantic night lying in each other's arms and looking at the stars while listening to Chicago's gorgeous love songs "For the Love" and "Memories of Love." We ended up being inspired to write a song together called "That One Summer Night."

"That One Summer Night"

Verse 1:

That one summer night

Alone on the beach

The stars were so bright and within our reach

The sight of each wave

Such a lovely view

In the sand we engrave

Together me and you

Verse 2:

That one summer night

Lying in the sand

It just felt so right

To be holding your hand

The touch of your lips

Pressed against mine

My heartbeat zipped

Dying to stop time

Verse 3:

That one summer night

Oh how I wish we had stayed

Under the moonlight

In the sand where we laid

With all the time passed

I long for that sight

My wish had been cast for that one summer night

We sat there and sang the melody together. We were both proud of our song and knew we would always remember our time together on the beach. As I got older, I started to cherish every moment. Before, I always took life for granted, but after I came back from the dead and with my grandfather dying, I started thinking differently. I wanted to make the most of everything and make as many special memories as possible on earth before making new memories in heaven.

CHAPTER 37: I'M A MAN

After we left LBI, it was finally time to play in the long-anticipated Sunlight Classic Game. There was a lot of hype going into the game. There were several articles about me, and one headline read, "Back from the dead and back onto the field!" The article talked about how much I overcame to be back playing football again. It was another inspirational article I put in my collection to save forever. Practices were so much fun, and I was very optimistic about the game.

Steph and I were on the couch watching *Rocky IV* on my game day when the phone rang. When my mom answered it, her happy expression vanished in an instant. When she got off the phone, she told me what had happened.

"It doesn't look great for Pop. He's fighting, but time is not on his side. He may only have a few days left."

We sat there in silence.

Finally, I breathed. "I have to go be with him. I have to go back to LBI. I can't play tonight."

My mom shook her head. "No, Drew. You worked for this moment your whole life. Daddy is with him now. Pop wants you to play. He told Daddy that he was watching you tonight. He is fighting to stay alive to watch you. Please let him see you play one more time. Dedicate this game to him. ."

I got choked up even more when she said that. I knew that I couldn't let him down. I wanted his last memory of me to be the best, so I had to play the greatest game of my life.

I dropped Steph off at home so she could prepare for the game, and then I went to my church, Saint Raphael's. Nobody was in the church, so I knelt, folded my arms, and prayed. I started talking to God. I first thanked Him for all He had given me and for helping me overcome everything that year. Then I asked Him to watch over my Pop. I didn't ask Him for a miracle but wanted God to be by His side in his final hours. I also asked Him to watch over me and help me to play a good game for my Pop.

"I've been telling everyone about our amazing meeting and spreading Your word like You told me. We have a lot of people on Your side fighting the good fight," I said while staring at the statue of Jesus on the cross.

Then, all of a sudden, I heard footsteps. When I turned, I saw Father Stan.

"Hi, Drew. Do you mind if I have a word?"

"Of course you can have a word," I said.

He sat down next to me and started talking. "So I heard your Grandpop isn't doing too well?"

I nodded. "No, not well at all. It's so hard for me to see him dying. He was always so upbeat and funny. I mean, I know heaven is an amazing place, but I'll miss him very much. I don't want to wait another 80 years to see him again," I said, with tears rolling down my face.

Father Stan solemnly smiled. He thought for a second, then looked back at me. "You don't have to wait 80 years. Your Pop will always be with you. Everywhere you go, you will be reminded of him. He is in your heart and your soul."

Then Father Stan stopped for a moment and started coughing.

"Are you okay, Father?" I asked him.

"Yes. I might be getting a little cold. But you have so many memories of your Pop; I know he's proud of you. The best part is that you know for a fact that there is a heaven and that Pop will be safe and happy up there. You know for a fact that you will see him again," he told me.

Father was right. So many people doubted heaven, and I knew for a fact that it was real. I knew that I would see my Pop again and that he would always be with me, just like Jesus would. I thanked Father very much and invited him to go to my game. He said he had some work to do, but he might try and finish up and catch it. He put his hand out to shake it, but I hugged him instead. I looked again at Jesus on the cross in the middle of the church and walked out, remembering that Jesus would always be with me.

As I walked out the church door, I put on my headphones and listened to the classic 80s song "Kyrie" by Mr. Mister. As I was listening to the song, getting pumped up for the game, I suddenly felt a massive punch to the back of my head. I then blacked out.

The next thing I knew, I was tied up to a pole in a run-down house. There was a tall vicious looking man with black hair standing in front of me. He was staring at me like he wanted to kill me and then he came right at me , punching me repeatedly.

"This is for beating up T-Rex!" He screamed while punching me.

"And now you're gonna die again and stay dead this time."

"You were the other guy that beat up Frankie, weren't you?" I asked him.

"Yes, I was, and I would have killed that loser if you didn't ruin everything," he growled.

He kicked my bad knee, but then he stopped punching me and said that he would be back to inflict more pain. A part of me knew that my life was going to be over again, and I thought that at least I would be with my Pop in heaven. But I wasn't ready to die yet. I had so much more life to live. I looked down at my cross necklace and remembered that Jesus told me He would always be my side. Jesus also told me He needed me on earth because I had to help Him fight evil. But He also said that sometimes evil prevails. I knew that I could not let evil prevail this time.

I was all alone, tied up, and beaten badly. Blood and tears were dripping down my eyes, and I could hardly see. I just kept imagining Steph's face. The man came back with a knife and started scraping my chest, causing me to bleed. It felt like a scene from one of my favorite Stallone movies, *Rambo: First Blood Part II*. My hands and feet were losing circulation because they were tied to the pole.

For a moment, I just wanted him to stab the knife in my heart and end my life because I was just so tired of fighting. But then everything changed in a moment when I heard a very familiar ringtone. It was the tin whistle melody that Timmy the Tin Whistler played at the hospital and on the plane to heaven.

The man who kidnapped me looked back at his phone." What the heck? That is not my ringtone," he said with a confused look on his face.

Then I heard and saw a plane out the window of the run-down house. I knew the wings in the sky were sending me a sign to fight evil.

The man hung up the phone, but the same tin whistle melody kept going off. It was getting louder and louder. I suddenly had so much more faith and strength. I felt stronger than ever and somehow could break the tie, holding down my feet. I just kept kicking and kicking until the tie came undone. I kept picturing driving my legs up the hill with the sled my dad made me do—all the workouts paid off.

The man panicked, so he threw his phone and came charging at me with a knife. I used the old martial arts that I had learned and kicked his knife away. I kept kicking him until he was knocked out unconscious. My hands were still tied, so I kept wiggling and freed them. I was bleeding and badly beaten up, but I knew that I had the Sunlight Classic game to catch because my Pop was fighting to stay alive to watch me. I quickly took the man's phone and called the Police. I couldn't find the keys to his car but did find a motorcycle with keys outside. I had never ridden one before but knew I had no choice. I also knew that I was in a violent part of Trenton.

As soon as I got on the bike, I saw a car of possible bad guys pull behind me. Without any warning, they took out guns and started to fire at me. I couldn't believe that there were more people involved with T-Rex. I figured that they must have been a gang. I drove as fast as I could to avoid the bullets. I was so scared, but I knew I just had to keep riding until I lost them. I was driving as fast as I could, and it was literally like an action chase from another one of my favorite Stallone movies, *Cobra*.

I was going so fast that I was able to avoid the bullets. For some reason, I could hear the Chicago rocker "Poem 58" playing in my head with Terry Kath's fast guitar as I rode the bike faster than ever. It was the craziest moment of my life because cars were beeping left and right. Then, all of a sudden, a massive truck cut off their car, and I was in the clear. I escaped by the skin of my teeth. I knew I was a few minutes away from my game, but I still had no idea what time it was. The crazy thing was that the plane was still flying over me, almost as if it was guiding me to the game.

I finally made it to the stadium without any cops even pulling me over. I had no time to park in the lot, so I rode my motorcycle onto the track, and the crowd went wild. Ironically, Chicago's hard rock song "I'm a Man" blasted in the stadium as I rode in. Everyone was stunned that I was on a motorcycle with blood pouring down my face, but I had no time to explain. I parked the bike and ran into the locker room.

I apologized to my team, telling them I got caught up in a shootout. They were confused, at the very least.

"Drew, you are bleeding and limping. I can't let you play like that. I have no idea what happened, but I can't," the Coach said.

So I did what I did best; I stood my ground." Coach, I just overcame being kidnapped and nearly beaten to death, not to mention I rode a motorcycle here and got shot at by gang members in a high-speed chase. I'm playing this game, or else you will have to drag me off this field."

Everyone was stunned. However, the coach recovered and was still trying to process what I told him. My dad and Steph came running in, and I told them what had happened. They were in shock, and Steph convinced me not to play. But she knew there was no use and that I had to play for Pop. Then I called the hospital where Pop was at. Grandmom answered, and I asked her to talk to Pop.

"Hey, Pop. How are you?"

"I've been better," he said in a feeble voice. Don't you have a game to play?"

"I do, Pop. I'm dedicating it to you. I have to go play now. But I love you so much."

"I love you too, Drew. I'll always love you and look after you. Jesus came to me in a dream last night and told me it was almost my time. He said to tell you to look for my signs. He also said something about His plane helping you escape a shootout."

I got chills because I knew that the plane was Jesus.

"It's time for me to go now. I'll see you again in about 80 years after you complete helping God spread His Word. I'll always love you, Goose Karate Kid," my Pop said, and I knew it was the last time I would ever speak to him on earth.

I put my helmet on my teary-eyed face and ran out of the stadium when they announced my name. They were blasting Chicago, singing my song "Ready to Stand," and I heard a huge applause from the crowd. I had so much pain in my body, but I didn't care. I was a fighter. I knew my enemies, Shane Hitt and

PJ Stanton, were all teaming up to take me down, but nobody would stop me. If I could break free from being kidnapped, tied up, and escape an attack of bullets, there was no way Hitt and Stanton were going to take me down.

CHAPTER 38: VICTORIOUS

The game was underway, and it would be my best game ever. Stanton and Hitt kept coming for me, and I juked them out every time. Every time I got the ball, I was still so angry from getting tied up and beaten that I refused to go down. I ran all over the East team and scored touchdowns left and right. I still had the adrenaline rush from the shootout and imagined the opposing players were bullets. I knew I could avoid any defender if I could avoid bullets.

At the end of the game, they passed me the ball on a screen pass, and I took it 66 yards for a touchdown to win the game. Right before I scored, I saw Hitt coming for me and thought about all of the times he was a jerk to me. I put every ounce of force and ran him over.

Then, the next guy to beat was Stanton, and I thought about him taking out my dad on the sideline with the cheapest shot ever, causing him to tear his ACL. I saw him coming on my left side and I decided to juke him out so badly that it caused him to fall. I then cruised my way into the end zone. Stanton actually got injured because I juked him out so much. Football players always joked around about juking out someone so much that it breaks their ankles and the funny thing was that I actually ended up breaking Stanton's ankle. He had to leave in an ambulance. I also caused Shane Hitt to get a concussion by running him over. It felt so great to get revenge on Hitt and Stanton after all they put me through.

I ended the game with over 200 yards and 4 touchdowns, all while beating my opponents again. Steph, Thomas, Allison, Lido, Frankie, my brothers, and my parents celebrated with me. It felt so good to come back from everything and have the people who had supported me there to watch me.

After the game, my dad told me that Pop was watching the whole time and slowly raised his hand excitedly every time I did something good. Grandmom said he was so proud and smiling from ear to ear. I won the MVP award, and I had a lot to say when it was time to give my speech.

"I want to dedicate this game to my beloved Grandpop in LBI. Pop, you were in my mind throughout this entire game. You are my inspiration and my hero. I love you more than anything and will always love you!"

According to Grandmom, Pop heard me say that and used all his strength to say he loved me, too.

Once the awards were over, the interviewers asked me many questions about what had happened earlier. I told them about the crazy events, and I knew that the media would be all over it.

All of my friends and family came down and were celebrating with me. After the ceremonies, I quickly removed my football equipment and drove with Steph to LBI to see Pop.

When we got to Pop's room, we saw my Grandmom by his side, holding his hand and crying. My aunt and uncle were also crying, and I knew it was too late. My Pop had boarded the plane to heaven.

Grandmom could not let go of his hand. I hugged her and cried in her arms.

"He used every ounce of strength to keep his promise of seeing your game, Drew. He even stayed alive long enough to see you dedicate the ball to him," my Grandmom told me while crying.

I knew that he would keep his promise. I knew where I got my ability to fight. Pop was such an inspiration. I couldn't believe that he was gone. I looked at his body and couldn't believe that he would never be able to be awake again on this earth. Our whole family sat there and just looked at Pop's lifeless body.

Soon, we started talking about the old days and sharing funny stories about him. It was reassuring and heartbreaking at the same time.

Just as we were about to leave Pop's room, I got a phone call from the Police telling me that the guy who had beaten me had escaped the house before they arrived. They also could not find the car that was chasing me. The cop assured me that they would keep looking and do whatever they could to catch them. They believed that they were all part of an extremely evil gang.

More terrible news came because then Thomas Simmons called me to tell me that Father Stan was rushed to the hospital. He was about to get in his car to go watch me play in the game and had a massive heart attack. Father Stan had been suffering from heart failure and was on the waiting list to receive a new heart. The crazy thing was that I found out that my Pop was an organ donor, and Father Stan was next on the list to receive a heart. He actually could be getting my Pop's heart. I could not believe it.

I couldn't believe any of the events that took place on that day. It was crazy and like something out of a movie, but I just needed to think that Pop would be looking over Father Stan and help his heart be a match.

Pop's heart ended up being a match, and they prepped Father Stan for surgery. The surgery ended up being a success, and my beloved Pop's heart was now in my beloved Father Stan's. When we were cleared to visit Father, I told him about my beloved Pop. While I was telling Father about him, Father Stan started to make a melody by tapping his hands on the table.

"What are you doing?" I asked him.

"I don't know, but I suddenly had the urge to start doing that," Father Stan said.

I told him that my Pop used to do that on the table all of the time. He told me to look for the signs that he was with us, and Father Stan was already showing signs. Pop will always live on forever in the hearts of all of us, especially in the heart of Father Stan.

CHAPTER 39: LOVE LIVES ON

We had a funeral for my Pop, and it was one of the most challenging days of my life. The hardest part was watching them put the lid of the casket over top of him and seeing my Grandmom sob. I was dealing with so many emotions. I did listen to the Chicago song "Love Lives On" for comfort because the lyrics fit. "Love lives on, with or without people in it, the path that follows has no limit, everything we do goes beyond, and even what we leave behind us, someday will come back to find us; I'm telling you that we're that strong, love lives on." I knew that my Pop's love would always live on.

I kept visiting Father Stan during that period. I told him that I was tired of all the media attention and that I wanted some alone time so that I could meditate and grieve alone. Steph had to go to visit her college for a few days, so Father Stan suggested that I take his keys to his retreat cabin in the Pocono Mountains. He said it would really help me think and feel God in nature. I thought it over and ended up going.

It was a beautiful cabin with no distractions. It just had the bible and lots of religious items in there. I took many walks around the mountains, and I could feel God in nature. I loved listening to Chicago's song "In the Country" because it was all about taking in the beauty of nature. I talked to God, and I spoke to Pop. Pop was a fabulous artist, and seeing the mountains reminded me of many of his mountain paintings. I asked Pop and Jesus to give me strength and guidance in the hard times when my life was changing. I was starting college in less than a month, and everything was happening so fast. I read the bible and tried to break it down and learn lessons from it.

I also got to do some great exercises. I had no equipment, so I took a chapter from *Rocky IV* and ran the mountains, threw rocks, carried logs, and chopped trees. I had such intense workouts while blasting the *Rocky IV* score songs like "Training Montage" and "War." Working out and praying made me feel much better. I was still worried that the men who kidnapped me were still out there, but I prayed that God would look after us. I also gave the police a complete description of the one man, so it was only a matter of time before they could find them.

I did miss Steph and couldn't wait to see her. All of my alone time and meditation helped me write a great song in honor of Pop. I called the song "Memory."

"Memory"

Verse 1:

It's been a tragedy, but I try to see

How to keep on moving fast and free

When go to cry

I realize all the tears and the joy in our eyes

Chorus:

You've given us all what we had to learn

It showed us life in a whole new world

And now that you're gone

We're still standing tall

Cause your memory will live in us all

Verse 2:

It's been hard for me

Cause I can't believe

How you left this earth so suddenly

But now I know

You're with Jesus in heaven forever

Chorus:

You've given us all what we had to learn

It showed us life in a whole new world

And now that you're gone

We're still standing tall

Cause your memory will live in us all

Bridge:

Although your body has died

Our memories with you

Will always be alive

Chorus:

You've given us all what we had to learn

It showed us life in a whole new world

And now that you're gone

We're still standing tall

Cause your memory will live in us all

Verse 3:

But now it's time

To say goodbye

I know it's hard, but we have to try

To move on with our lives

And I know someday we'll meet again

But until then

Our memories will live till the end

Chorus:

You've given us all what we had to learn

It showed us life in a whole new world

And now that you're gone

We're still standing tall

Cause your memory will live in us all

We were all so blessed to have had Pop for as many years as we had him, and although he was gone, his memory and his spirit would live on in his family, friends, and Father Stan's heart forever. I knew that I would see him again one day on board the wings in the sky.

CHAPTER 40: HAPPY MAN

I also wrote another new song called, "A Thousand Reasons." I was proud of this song because, like "Ready to Stand," it defined my past year.

"A Thousand Reasons"

Verse 1:

You've been hit with such a hard blow

And you feel like there's nowhere to go

You've lost your faith in the world and your faith in God

But you have to go on

Cause you are way too strong

Chorus:

And there are a thousand reasons

Why you can't give up

A thousand reasons

You are way too tough

There's no reason to throw in the towel

So take a vowel to have faith in God and believe

Cause there are a thousand reasons why you can succeed

Verse 2:

You've fallen down to the ground

And you feel like you can't turn your life around

But it's time to dig down deep

And wake up from your sleep

And you have to go on cause you are way too strong

Chorus:

And there are a thousand reasons

Why you can't give up

A thousand reasons

You are way too tough

There's no reason to throw in the towel

So take a vowel to have faith in God and believe

Cause there are a thousand reasons why you can succeed

Bridge:

I know you have really lost your way

But you have so much more life to live

So find your faith in yourself

And God today

Chorus:

And there are a thousand reasons

Why you can't give up

A thousand reasons

You are way too tough

There's no reason to throw in the towel

So take a vowel to have faith in God and believe

Cause there are a thousand reasons why you can succeed

If people stop feeling sorry for themselves and start to dig deep and find their strength and their faith, they can accomplish anything. I sat on the top of the mountain listening to Peter Cetera's *The Karate Kid Part II* theme song, "Glory of Love," and thought hard about all the things that happened in the past year.

Then I remembered Mr. Stevens and my father talking about the Stone of Sisyphus and how everybody is like Sisyphus. We all fall down the hill, and I fell several times that year, but I learned so many things from my failures, successes, friends, family, and tragedies.

For the first time in my life, I was starting to become a man. Before, I was just a spoiled young kid. But I was finally given obstacles to overcome, and I was able to overcome them. They were not just everyday teenage obstacles either, like overcoming getting dumped by a girl. They were overcoming death and being kidnapped. I also learned so much from my friends Frankie and Lido and how strong they were. So many people had inspired me; hopefully, I inspired them, too. I knew that I was at the end of my childhood and the beginning of my adulthood.

I then decided to go back to the cabin. As I headed back, I smelled fried chicken, which smelled delicious. I had yet to learn where it was coming from. I opened the door and was surprised to see that my beloved Steph was there cooking in the kitchen. She gave me a kiss square on the lips, and Chicago's power ballad "You're Not Alone" was playing loudly.

Although it was nice to be alone for a few days to meditate and reflect, I missed Steph so much, and I was so happy to see her. We had a very romantic dinner and then relaxed on the couch. After we relaxed, we had a hard workout outside and ran up the mountain several times. After we ran, we relaxed by sitting high on the mountain top. We held hands and just looked down, taking in the beauty of nature while listening to Chicago's "Happy Man." I knew that despite the hardships, I was a very happy man. I took my phone out and pulled up the picture of me lying at the bottom of the hill on the night that Frankie was attacked. I remembered that I vowed never to stop fighting to get back to the top that night. I was so happy that I kept my promise. I then took a picture of me and Steph sitting at the top of the mountain so that I would remember how incredible it felt to be on top.

I smiled. "I am so lucky to sit up here with you, Steph. Although I was on the bottom of the hill a lot this year, I am truly on top now, thanks to you. You are my inspiration, and I would still be at the bottom without you," I told her.

She shook her head. "No, Drew. It was your toughness and your heart that got you to the top. You are the strongest person I know."

I had tears in my eyes because I felt like the heavens were looking down on us as we were sitting on top of the mountain.

I looked down and knew that I was eventually going to fall again, especially with the horrible guys who kidnapped me still being out there. It was inevitable, but I knew that with the help of Steph, my parents, Father Stan, and my friends, I could get back to the top.

Then, all of a sudden, I could hear a tin whistle melody from heaven, and Steph actually could hear it too. We heard a plane, looked up, and sure enough, there was one right above us. I knew that it was Pop on the plane flying with Jesus.

I then vowed to Steph that I would rise back up to the top of the mountain every time that I would fall. I promised never to stay at the bottom, and Steph pledged that she would always be by my side to help me. Steph was getting tired and asked me if I was ready to stand and go back in. We both held each other's hands and stood on top of the hill, looking all the way down. I wasn't sure when I would fall again, but I knew that when I eventually fell to the bottom, I would always be ready to stand.

Acknowledgments

Writing this book has been a journey filled with countless moments of gratitude and reflection. I owe a debt of thanks to the remarkable individuals who have touched my life in profound ways and made this endeavor possible.

First and foremost, I extend my deepest appreciation to my beloved wife, Stephanie Fuccello. Your unwavering love and support have been my rock throughout this entire process. Your encouragement and understanding have illuminated my path, guiding me through every twist and turn.

To my parents, Jim Fuccello Sr. and Gloriann Fuccello, I am forever grateful for the values of perseverance and determination you instilled in me from an early age. Your belief in my abilities has served as a constant source of strength and motivation. I would not be the athlete I am today without my father being my personal trainer since I was 6 years old.

To my brothers, Frankie and Nicky Fuccello, your steadfast support and camaraderie have been a beacon of inspiration. Together, we have weathered life's storms and celebrated its triumphs, forging an unbreakable bond along the way.

My heartfelt gratitude extends to my PopPop, Frank Capasso, whose wisdom and guidance have been invaluable, and to my sister-in-law, Breanna Fuccello, my niece Jaclynn Fuccello, and Dena Parmigiani, for their encouragement.

I am deeply thankful for the love and support of my cousin, Christopher Fuccello, Aunt Chris Fuccello, Uncle Frankie

Fuccello, Aunt Helen Furman, Uncle Ted Furman, Aunt Marcie Rossidivito, Aunt Elena Roman, Uncle John Roman, and Aunt Paula Ferguson.

To my dear friends Julianne Clark, Kelly Walsh, Chelsea Maguire, Nancy Duffy, Adelaide Mcelroy-Torpila, Kim Smith, Matt Wallace, and Nick Gomberg, your amazing friendship and encouragement have lifted me up during the most challenging moments of this journey.

Special thanks are extended to my sister-in-law Elyse Moceri, brother-in-law Jeff Moceri, mother-in-law Robin Moceri, father-in-law Brian Moceri, and Cindy Moceri for their tremendous support.

I owe a debt of gratitude to the school where I teach Physical Education, Saint Raphael School, and my former high school, Notre Dame High School in Lawrenceville, NJ, for providing me with a nurturing environment where I could grow and thrive. Thank you to former Notre Dame Coach Chappy Moore. Special thanks to my Saint Raphael students, whom I am so honored to get to teach every day. Thank you to all of my incredible teachers who I had throughout my lifetime, especially Mr. John Wojcik.

I want to express my heartfelt gratitude to the iconic band Chicago for providing the soundtrack of my life and crafting songs that continue to inspire me daily. A special acknowledgment goes to Jason Scheff, the lead singer for three decades, for his countless support and friendship. I also extend my thanks to Sylvester Stallone and his timeless *Rocky* movies, which have served as a constant source of inspiration for me.

In loving memory of Frank Fuccello Sr., Helen Fuccello, Marie Capasso, Nicholas G. Capasso, Coach John McKenna, Dan Bartram, and sports writer George O'Gorman whose legacies inspire me daily.

Made in the USA
Columbia, SC
19 June 2024

5685bc16-f778-4b2c-b6b6-9c0133d39aacR01